I0609801

Body at the Beach

Holly Holcraft Mysteries, Volume 3

M R Dollschnieder

Published by M R Dollschnieder, 2025.

Also by M R Dollschnieder

Holly Holcraft Mysteries
Bones in the Backyard
Fear at the Fall Festival
Body at the Beach

AN INVITATION

"One of my friends is letting me use their beach house for the weekend. Can you come?" Lucy's question Thursday night seemed ridiculous right off the bat as I sat bundled up in warm furry blankets in front of the fireplace where a cozy fire sparked and crackled. Lucy White is our local title representative and, more importantly, one of my best friends. The more I thought about it, the more it sounded wonderful. Just us on the beach watching the surf and then falling asleep at night to the sounds of the waves crashing on the shore. No worries over getting files finished or home inspections in the snow. No frozen pipes. I glanced over to the window where I could see big fluffy flakes of snow drifting down to land on the bushes outside. Winter had just begun here in Appleby, our little mountain town, but it had been freezing for more than a month.

"Holly, you still there?"

"Yes, beach, definitely. When do we leave?" I asked, looking forward to a peaceful weekend laying on the sand and getting some sun. This old body of mine definitely needed some sunshine.

"Tomorrow morning early. Shelby and Vana are coming too."

"Sounds like it's gonna be epic." I'd also known Vana Dago for ten years. I'd met both her and Lucy when I moved here after losing my husband in a car accident. Shelby White, no relation to Lucy, and I had gone to high school together. She is the one that encouraged me to move here. It was her telling me about how beautiful it was up here and how friendly everyone was that convinced me to come.

I'm a real estate agent and I've made a living here selling and reselling properties to people who love the area and then can't handle the winter or the influx of seasonal tourists. It takes a special kind of person to live here in our small mountain community of Appleby.

It truly is beautiful up here, all the seasons have their special attributes. Even winter with the snow and icy roads. There is something so peaceful and quiet about a snow covered valley that can't be found anywhere else. It's like a giant blanket that muffles all sound while looking gloriously beautiful.

"Great. Vana will pick you up and then come get me. We're gonna fly out of Morecroft so we can spend the most time at the beach. Be ready, 5 am sharp!" I could feel the enthusiasm in her voice rub off on me. I'm not really a morning person so I packed my clothes and prepped everything so tomorrow all I have to do is stumble around half asleep and get dressed. I made arrangements with my daughter, Penelope, to check in on my dog Ginger. Thanks to my neighbor, Ben Brown, installing a rolling bar at the top of my back fence that curtailed Ginger's escapes from the backyard, I felt safe leaving the doggy door out so she could come and go as she pleased.

Although, she had saved me and Mildred Beaumont, the candy store owner, once by jumping over the fence. Okay, the guy was already unconscious on the ground but still, it's the thought that counts. Ginger is a 70 pound Shepherd-Doberman mix and I hadn't even known she was getting out until Ben let me know she'd been visiting him and his dog Bernard. No one will break into my house with Ginger here. She's an excellent guard dog.

After a second glance around, I turned off the lights and climbed into bed. Ginger was already there dreaming little doggy dreams and I soon joined her in sleep.

FLIGHT

The airport in Morecroft is pretty small and we found ourselves looking at the small commercial aircraft we would soon be flying in. I surveyed the small light planes, which constituted most of the airport traffic, lined up along the runway waiting for the owners to take a flight. Considering it's nearly winter, this was probably their home for the next short while. Winter storms can get pretty gnarly out here in the mountains.

Our plane was bigger than the private planes but not by much. "Uh, you sure this plane is going to get us to our destination?" I asked worriedly as an icy wind gusted by us on our way to the terminal. We had all peeled off our heavy jackets and left them in the car so we wouldn't have to lug them with us at the beach. Now we were making a rapid dash through the frigid air to the terminal door in our jeans and sweaters while pulling our wheelie bags. Vana as usual had two.

Shelby waved her graceful hand through the air. She is tall and thin with gorgeous dark brown hair and looks great in everything she wears, which today was a navy blue turtleneck and dark blue jeans. "Of course it is, I fly these all the time," she said huffing. Shelby is forthright to a fault so her confidence in the plane eased my fears a little. It was 7 am and the overcast sky had finally begun to lighten. We slipped through the door into the warm air of the terminal which felt like heaven. I shivered a few times in the warm air, shaking off the outdoor cold, as we took our place on the hard plastic seats in the small terminal to wait for our boarding call.

"They serve wine on board right?" asked Vana. Vana was the sister I always wanted. I think we just got each other. Plus she had the sweetest husband. It was early, but I agreed with her. Sometimes alcohol is necessary during a flight. Particularly when you are flying over tall mountains in a tiny plane. The stewardess called our flight a few moments later, so we checked our luggage and found seats next to each other. The plane had two seats on either side with an aisle in the middle so Vana and I sat together across from Lucy and Shelby. The seats in the plane were definitely more comfortable than the hard seats we had been sitting on.

Once the plane was airborne, Vana twisted to look at me. "I've got a great idea. If we look at open houses while we're there, we can write the trip off as a tax deduction."

I frowned at her. Something about that idea made me think she had it planned all along. "Are you sure about that? I just paid my taxes, I don't want to open another can of worms." I'd been audited before and I hadn't enjoyed it.

"Yes, as long as we keep our receipts and document the houses we go to. We can't deduct everything but enough."

Shelby leaned forward to see me past Vana. "How much time is that going to take? I want to spend as much time as possible by the water."

"Oh come on girls. You know we're not going to spend the entire time on the sand anyway, we'll be fried," I said. Who wouldn't want to look at gorgeous million dollar homes by the beach? I imagined multilevel stories with fantastic views of the ocean in homes with floor to ceiling windows.

Lucy twisted her lips. "Okay, maybe just one or two as long as they're by the beach and have a great view."

"Awesome!" chortled Vana. "I already have a few picked out." Of course she did.

"A few?" I whispered in her ear.

"Don't worry about it, it'll be fun. Just think, sun, sand and no murders."

"Don't jinx it for us." I made the sign of the cross before settling back into my seat and watching the clouds float by below us. Until recently, my life in Appleby had been going rather smoothly. it had been a wonderful place to raise my now adult daughter, Penelope. It was just me and Ginger now, cruising by in life until my client, Carol Oates, was accused of killing her husband. The dead pig in her garage didn't help matters.

Of course, I had to help her. Then I found out a longtime acquaintance was responsible for my husband's fatal car accident. Fortunately, she had been arrested recently and would finally be punished for her crimes. And then a few weeks ago, the Fall Festival I chaired was marred by the death of a friend all because of a treasure that had been lost for fifty years. Heck It might be lost for another fifty years. That made me think of the finger bone I had found in my client's garage mixed amongst the muck from the dead pig. It had been 10,000 years old and Carol had turned out to be an actual archeologist. At the time I'd wanted nothing to do with sleuthing but it was beginning to appeal to me. After all, it was just another way of helping people. Of course, I'm not about to admit that to anyone.

"Hey, daydreamer," called Shelby. "What're you thinking about?" I looked up to see all three of the girls staring at me.

"We've been discussing our plans and you've been off in la la land," added Lucy.

"I'm sorry, I was just thinking about lost treasure and that finger bone we found. You know, all unresolved mysteries," I said.

Shelby's eyes widened. "I thought you didn't like sleuthing."

"Oh no. She's embraced it now," confided Vana. "She actually likes it, I can tell." So much for keeping it a secret. The look on her face showed she didn't agree with my new found passion.

Lucy waved her finger back and forth in my direction. "Oh, no, no, no,no. We are not getting involved in any mysteries, murders or any other sort of mayhem. This is a relaxing weekend on the beach with friends. Agreed?"

"Of course," I responded. "Relaxing, beach, friends. Got it." I settled back into my seat and looked out the window. We were flying over fluffy clouds that resembled fat sheep meandering across the landscape.

"Hmph," snorted Vana. "You know these things just seem to happen to her lately." She looked at me doubtfully.

"Well we're not having it this time," snapped Shelby and then sat back in her seat as if the whole matter was settled. Well, I hope she's right because I really do want to just enjoy the scenery and a few open houses. Of course, it's not my fault if someone needs some assistance. I glanced up to another glare from Vana and shrugged my shoulders while looking as innocent as possible.

The landing at the airport went without incident and we picked up our car rental from a booth in the terminal. It was a light blue 2024 Honda Prologue with a digital display. "Vana, are you sure you're okay to drive this? I know how you like your buttons." I like to tease her because she always insists on driving and also, if you have ever had her as a back seat driver, you would let her drive too.

"Very funny," she shot back.

"Okay," I said, "but I better not see you looking at that display. Tell me what you want and I'll do it." At this Lucy and Shelby laughed because I am the least technologically savvy of all of us. I stuck my bottom lip out and pretended to pout. Totally ignoring me, Vana started the car and then punched in the address to the beach house which turned out to be less than 45 minutes from the airport.

Our drive was filled with traffic and we spent more time sitting at red lights than I care to count. The streets were narrow, which was surprising considering how big cars used to be back then. Small houses from the forties and fifties lined the streets. They were all packed in next to each other with tiny little front yards.The closer we got to our destination, the newer and larger the homes became. When we arrived at the beach house I was pleasantly surprised to see that it was one of the newer ones.

The beach house was fantastic. Leave it to Lucy to know affluent people. It was two levels situated on stilts for high tide with a staircase going down to the beach. The balcony railings were made out of glass so the view wouldn't be obstructed. I could sit out here all day, just watching the waves roll in.

"Now this is what I'm talking about," declared Shelby. We were all standing at the balcony looking out at the beach below us. "Great views, huge windows and comfy furniture. Plus, I remembered my binoculars."

"Men watching," we all said in unison and then laughed. Shelby was notoriously man crazy. Hopefully, she wouldn't be too difficult on this short trip. After getting settled in our rooms, we slipped into our swimsuits and made our way down to the beach for some relaxation. Our bare feet sank into the soft sand. It being Friday morning, there were more birds on the beach than people. Off to the left was the harbor and on the right was a pier with some local shops and restaurants.

The sky was overcast, but already the clouds were thinning and I could see blue sky periodically. Compared to Appleby, it felt positively balmy even without the sunshine. Actually, anything over 50 degrees feels warm now when you're used to 32 and below.

"It should clear up this afternoon," commented Lucy looking at the sky. "It always does." We found a nice section of sand to spread out our towels and plopped down. "Did anyone bring sunscreen?" I asked to no avail, kicking myself mentally for not thinking of it.

Vana laid down on her back and closed her eyes. "You'll be fine. The sun's not even out."

"You can still get sunburned on a cloudy day," I protested.

"We'll get some when we get lunch," added Shelby from where she lay on her towel with her eyes closed.

As the air warmed, the beach began to fill with sunbathers, families with kids digging in the sand with toys, surfers, and dogs chasing balls. Time drifted by to the sound of the crashing waves and the shrieks of the seagulls. It was so relaxing, and I'd gotten up so early that I dozed off.

"STOP TOUCHING IT." Lucy slapped my hand away from my shoulder. It was two hours later and my finger left a white spot on my pink shoulder when I pressed down on it.

"How could you forget the sunscreen?" I whined. "I'm a crispy critter."

"Who thinks of sunscreen in the winter? We can stop and get some on our way to look at the houses. Plus, you'll have everybody at home jealous," added Vana.

Shelby poked my shoulder with her finger. "Does it hurt?"

"Well, no," I admitted. "At least not yet."

"Great," said Vana. "We'll get sunscreen and you'll be fine. Now this first house I found sits up on the hillside about a half mile from the beach. That'll be a great view for you Lucy. It's four bedrooms, two bathrooms and it's a split level like this one."

Excited about getting to see some beautiful beach homes, we quickly threw on a change of clothes and joined Vana in the car. After putting on her seatbelt, she leaned over and punched in the address on the navigation system of our rental car. "We should be there in about ten minutes."

OPEN HOUSE

The ten minutes turned into twenty due to the traffic congestion, but still, twenty minutes to the beach is not bad. I wasn't getting a good feeling about the open house as the closer we got, the smaller and closer together the houses became. Where were the big split levels Vana promised us? Where would Ginger run in a yard like these? I felt sorry for any animals that lived here. I focused my attention back on the digital display. Since I was sitting shotgun, I was the designated navigator.

"Turn at this gas station here," I said, indicating the one coming up on my right. My seatbelt lightened uncomfortably against my shoulder as a woman in a beige Mercedes cut across our lane to make the corner and caused Vana to slam on the brakes. After saying a few inappropriate words, she took a couple deep breaths and continued on to the sound of honking behind her.

"Of all the nerve," exclaimed Shelby, before adding, "if I was going to drive a Mercedes, it would definitely be a red one. Why spend all that money on a car and get boring beige?"

"Yes," breathed Vana. "The choice of color of the crazy woman's car is the thing to focus on right now. Why yes, I am fine. Thank you for asking."

Shelby glanced over at her and rolled her eyes. "Oh Vana, of course I worry about you, but I can see you're fine and from the language you used, you're definitely not having a heart attack."

"Point taken," she said grudgingly although her body posture implied she was still annoyed.

The tree lined street led up through the little 1940's houses until we got to the top of the hill where the open house was tucked away against the hillside. The front yard was also tiny and I imagined there wasn't much back yard if any. Beach property is at a premium though and you've got the whole beach to play on. It had a shingle roof and tiny windows.

"Um, this is not like the beach house." Lucy pursed her lips as she peered out the car window.

"I said it was a split level, like the beach house." Vana clarified as she pulled into the angled driveway and parked. There was one car next to us, which I assumed belonged to the realtor. The garage was on the ground floor with two levels above. There were a few large trees providing shade and some bushes around the perimeter of the yard which provided a nice privacy screen for the house.

Lucy narrowed her eyes at Vana suspiciously. "The next ones had better be better."

We walked up the stairs to the front door and knocked. The slight breeze in the shade made me shiver.

"Would you look at that?" marveled Shelby turning in a circle. "You were right. The view is magnificent.

I turned to look. The land fell away from the hillside we were on and the town spread out below us, houses running all the way to the beach. Sunlight glistened on the water that reached to the horizon. "And that's why this property is two million dollars," said Vana. Lucy whistled in admiration. I looked down at my sunburned arms and my sundress and sandals.

"Do you think we're dressed okay?" I whispered.

"Pshaw, millionaires don't get dressed all fancy anymore," said Vana. "They dress in torn jeans and t-shirts like the rest of us. Come on, let's go in." Vana actually had a suit jacket on, Shelby was wearing jeans and a dress shirt and Lucy looked like a knock out as usual in a pretty summer dress. None of them had any pink on their skin. In fact, it looked suspiciously darker than mine.

No one had ever answered our knock so we tried the door which was unlocked. "Hellooo, real estate agents. Anyone here?" Vana's call was met with silence but these things happen all the time. The agent was probably just in another room.

"You're sure this is the house right?" I asked.There hadn't been any open house signs and there were no flyers or cookies. I always have cookies at open houses.

"Uh huh. I even called to confirm. They're in here somewhere."

For a million dollar home, it was pretty boring by anyone's standards. There was a small mudroom and bath next to the garage, then the kitchen and living room with a bath on the next level and the bedrooms with another bath on the top floor. The rooms were small and it hadn't been updated in decades. Except for the view, there wasn't anything special about it. It was decorated in mid-century modern. Pictures of what I assumed were the owner's family adorned the walls. There were a few blank spots where pictures used to be, I assumed because they were in the process of packing.

Shelby began opening drawers. "What are you doing? You can't look through people's things," I whisper shouted at her.

"What?" she shrugged. "I see people do it all the time."

"Cabinets and closets, not dressers and things that belong to the owners."

"Well, sorry, I didn't know." She peered into the drawer before closing it. "Oh, look, it's today's paper," she said, pulling it out and unfolding it.

I snatched the paper from Shelby and went to put it back in the drawer until I noticed it was open to the obituaries. You know, you can get great leads on houses and apartments from the obituaries.

"Holly! What are you doing? Put that back." Lucy admonished me as she peered over my shoulder at the paper. "Hey, isn't that the woman on the wall in the hallway?"

"Oh my God is this her house?" questioned Shelby. She always was afraid of ghosts

which is why she was conveniently absent during our Fall Festival.

"Whose house?" asked Vana, who had been paying no attention whatsoever to the conversation.

"The woman in the paper that died," squeaked Shelby. "Did she die here? I'm leaving."

"People die in houses all the time, you just don't know about it. A house this old may have had multiple people die in here by now."

Shelby's face looked white. "Vana, stop it. Shelby, there's no such thing as ghosts and she probably died in a hospital," I said.

Vana paused to open another drawer.

"Would you stop already! It's someone else's stuff," I admonished her. "Now, cupboards I can understand."

"Okay, fine. Let's look in this closet." Vana grabbed the handle behind her and pulled the door open without looking. Our eyes became huge as a hand landed on Vana's shoulder. She twisted her head sideways to peer at her shoulder where the hand was now resting. Screaming, she smacked it off her shoulder and then ducked to the side. A large male body fell to the floor landing face up with eyes staring at nothing. We all stared down at the man who had dark hair and a full mustache and beard. He appeared to be middle aged with a significant beer belly and was dressed in a plaid shirt and khaki shorts. Shelby dashed for the front door while Vana, Lucy and I stared at each other until I broke the silence.

"Where's the agent? We need to let her know."

"Oh that, um, the agent told us not to go through the cupboards, sorry I forgot to tell you," said Vana grimacing. Sure, she forgot.

"Somebody should make sure he's dead," I said. If I suggested it, then someone else had to do it right? That's what I was going with anyway. Vana and Lucy looked at me, then at the body, then at each other and shook their heads.

"No way. Besides, his eyes are open. That means he's dead right?" whispered Vana.

Lucy shrugged, "in the crime shows I watch it does."

"Maybe he just had a stroke and he's catatonic," whispered Vana.

"Is he breathing?" I asked. We all three stared at his chest but try as we might, we couldn't detect any motion. His sightless eyes continued to stare at the ceiling. Vana finally crept over and poked his cheek.

"He's pretty cold and he was pretty stiff when he fell," she added.

Making a decision I grabbed Lucy and Vana's arms and dragged them back to the front porch. Shelby was nowhere to be seen. I pulled the door closed behind us. "Let's just pretend we weren't here."

"We can't do that. Somebody just got murdered." Vana had her phone out and was punching in a number.

"I don't know what you're talking about, I didn't see anything," I replied innocently.

"How do we know that?" questioned Lucy. "He could have died of natural causes."

"He was in the closet!" Vana protested, pointedly looking at us as we tried to avoid her gaze.

"If you call the police our vacation is over and didn't you have more houses you wanted to see? Tax deductions and all that business?" I asked hopefully.

"Can I help you ladies?" called a pleasant voice from the driveway, and we all jumped. A blonde haired, middle aged woman in a beige two piece pantsuit, who was clearly a real estate agent, was just exiting her car and looking up at us still standing on the porch.

"Hi." I called down to her. "We're real estate agents here to see the house."

"That's great," she answered. "Just let me grab a few things from my car and I'll let you in. Have you been waiting long?" We all glanced at each other with wide eyes.

"Oh, no, not long at all," said Lucy.

As the agent leaned back into her car, I whispered, "Look, we'll just follow her in and express surprise when we find the dead guy. Again." I turned and smiled at her as she came up the stairs.

"Is your friend in the car going to join us?"

I looked at the car and could now see Shelby through the side window. She was frantically motioning to us to leave. "Oh, she's not feeling well. Too much sun today." Shelby glared at me through the car window.

"Well come on in. I'm Audrey Nicholson. This house is a great steal. The owner recently passed away. Oh, not in the house," she added quickly. "The family just wants it sold fast." She took a few moments in the house to quickly and efficiently set out her sign in sheet and business cards, then gave us each a flyer with a description of the home and I handed her my card. I barely listened as she led us from room to room highlighting the details.

"...And this is the master bedroom. Only because it's slightly bigger than the other room. It doesn't have its own bathroom or anything. When the house was built that wasn't a priority." She stepped inside the small room with the body on the floor and I cringed waiting for the scream which never came. Vana, Lucy and I glanced at each other and then peered through the doorway.

The closet door was shut and the floor was clear. There was no sign of a body. Vana stepped over to the closet. "Oh, this place is just so charming," she said as she grabbed the handle with a flourish and pulled the door open, making sure to stay to the side.

An empty closet greeted us. With a puzzled look, she glanced inside.

"Really," said an indignant Audrey, "the listing specifically says not to open the cabinets."

Vana was still looking in the closet when she answered. "I'm so sorry, I completely forgot. And technically this is a closet, not a cabinet."

"I'm sorry, I'm going to have to ask you to leave. If you can't respect a simple wish I don't think that I want to deal with you." she said as she ushered us back out onto the front porch and then shut the door in our faces.

Shelby yelled at us as soon as we shut the car doors. "What were you doing in there? You've been gone for half an hour. Someone is dead in there."

"No they're not," said Vana.

"Yes, they are. I saw the body," cried Shelby in frustration. "I told you these things fall into her lap." She waved her hand vigorously in my direction.

"That's just it," said Vana. "There isn't a body. It's gone. I couldn't even see any blood or anything in the closet."

"Hey," I said suddenly. "That's not the same car that was here when we pulled in."

"Are you sure?" asked Lucy.

"Can we puleeze get out of here?" whined Shelby.

"Yeah. That one is a Toyota Camry and the other one was a Honda Prelude. I know because Penelope has been car shopping and keeps sending me pictures of them. Was there a car parked next to us when you came outside?" We all turned to look at Shelby.

"There couldn't have been now, could there be if the agent pulled in next to us and parked." We exchanged frightened glances.

"The murderer was in the house with us and took the body when we left?" whispered Lucy.

"Can we leave now?" pleaded Shelby.

As Vana drove away, I took a moment to think. "Shelby, how did you not see someone drive the car away?"

Her face flushed red. "I didn't get in the car right away. I walked down the road a bit and when I came back it was gone."

"Had to be a man," declared Lucy suddenly.

"What?" we all asked.

"It had to be a man. We were only arguing for a short time. Only a strong man could carry the body out and dump it in the trunk before we got there."

"And I have a date for you," said Lucy.

"Wait, what?" The sudden shift threw me off and it took a moment for my brain to catch up. "You have a date for me here at the beach? When did you plan that? We're only here for two days." My voice rose in a panicked wail at the end. Seriously, what was she thinking?

"Because I know somebody, who knows somebody. He's a great guy, his name's Barry and I think you'll like him. So I think you should give it a try." At the look of reluctance on my face, she added. "C'mon Holly. You agreed I could pick your next date."

"Come on, you haven't had a serious relationship in ten years," added Vana.

I threw up my hands in defeat. "Okay, fine. I'll go on a date with Larry,"

"Barry," Lucy corrected me.

"Barry," I repeated.

"Don't be like those men and say the wrong name in bed," Shelby chided, apparently feeling better since we'd left the scene of the crime.

"Fine," I sighed. "I'll give it a try."

"Remember, you promised me that you would do it."

"I know, I know. I said I'll go. I don't know what you're expecting though since I live hours away by plane."

She shrugged her shoulders. "You just need to get back into practice. I'll expect a full report when you get back with all the juicy details."

"Ditto," said Shelby. I watched Vana roll her eyes through the rear view mirror. Of course she would. The dating bar she set was so low, people tripped over it.

"It's just going to dinner. It'll be great."

We rode back to the beach house in silence, the other open houses forgotten. As Vana pulled into the driveway I spoke up. "What if he wasn't dead. Maybe he was faking and ran away when we left the room. You said you didn't see any blood in the closet. Maybe he did it to scare us away."

Shelby looked suddenly happier. "That would be a relief because then we wouldn't have to worry about a murderer identifying us."

The four of us exchanged shocked looks. "I hadn't actually thought about that," said Lucy slowly. "Here's to hoping the guy was faking being dead."

"Great," said Vana. "So are we getting out or what? That sun isn't going to stay up all day." Without waiting for a response, she gathered her things and went to the trunk of the car where she pulled out an umbrella.

"You had that the whole time and didn't tell me?" I shrieked.

"Yeah, well, I didn't think we would need it until tomorrow. You really need to get out and get some sunshine," she said to me.

"In the dead of winter," was all I could think to respond. "Where do you suggest I work on my tan in the snow?"

"There's a tanning salon in Morecroft. I passed it the other day," said Lucy.

Shelby's eyes widened. "Really? I might need to go there. Do you remember the name?"

"Ladies!" said Vana as she slammed the trunk shut. "Talk and walk. Times a wastin.'" The three of them turned and walked toward the house. As I followed I couldn't help but think about Shelby's comment about the murderer. Did the person see us? Was the guy really dead? It seemed like a typical guy prank except, he never jumped up and laughed at us. That bothered me more than anything because the alternative was too horrible to contemplate.

BERNIE

Twenty minutes later, we were back in our swimsuits and settling ourselves on the beach, blonde, blue eyed me under the umbrella. The sand was warm and the sunlight sparkled off the waves as they crashed onshore. It was perfect. I stretched out on the towel and snuggled down into the sand. It was just the right amount of warm.

"Vana, you should call that agent back and apologize and maybe you could find out more information about the owner. She died but she didn't look that old."

Vana threw her hat at me. "Really Holly? We're on va-ca-tion."

Lucy piped up from the other side of Vana. "You really should apologize though, don't you think?" She was looking gorgeous in an orange bikini.

"You too?" Her voice sounded incredulous.

"I missed out on all the fun with the other cases. You know Holly, you could have asked me to help with the Fall Festival. I would have loved to see the bear."

This time I rolled my eyes. Sitting up on my elbow I directed my comment in her direction. "Maybe we'll run into a bear during the Yuletide Christmas Tour of Homes. Thanks for volunteering. Shelby, you want to help too? And then if any dead bodies turn up, I'll point them in your direction."

"Wait, wait, I wasn't complaining," protested Shelby.

"Too late, you're all helping this time. You too Vana. I skewered them all with my eyes before laying back down."

"Fine. I'll make the call."

We all listened in as she spoke to the agent but didn't get much from the one-sided conversation. Hanging up she said, "you're never going to believe this."

At her words we all sat up. Shelby's floral patterned one piece hugged her in all the right places. Why couldn't I look like that in a swimsuit? Vana and I were both wearing one pieces that covered us in all the right places. "That woman we met wasn't the agent. Somebody stole her car while she was putting up open house signs. She found her car in the driveway and the front door unlocked. The house was ransacked. Audrey, that really is her name, said the owner was 47 and died from cancer. Apparently she'd been suffering with it for a while. She asked if we'd give a statement to the police."

For a long while afterwards, no one said a word. Shelby finally said, "of course we will."

"Are you sure Shelby? You were pretty freaked out," asked Vana.

"Yes I'm sure," she said in an angry voice. "I'm tired of people being jerks and lying."

"Shelbs, you okay?" asked Lucy. "You've been out of sorts lately. Is it the lack of sunlight?"

"Oh. It's not the hormones again is it?" I asked, suddenly concerned. Shelby's hormones had caused us to be kicked out of a bar. I didn't really want to go through that again.

Shelby hugged her knees and buried her head in her arms. "I think I'm going through m....," she mumbled.

"What?" we all asked but only because she was mumbling. She picked her head up and said loudly, "Men-O-pause okay? I'm getting old," and she burst into tears. "My hair is going to get all thin and yucky and I'm going to get fat," she wailed.

I threw my sandal at her head. "What was that for?" she yelled.

"Are you fat and do you have yucky hair now?" I asked.

She sniffled. "No."

"Menopause isn't a death sentence and there are things you can do to reduce the symptoms."

"Really?" she asked hopefully.

Vana handed her a tissue. "What did the doctor say?"

Shelby bit her lip. "I didn't ask. I, I Googled it."

This time Lucy threw her shoe at her. "Really Shelby. When we get back you're making an appointment."

"But I have all the symptoms," she protested.

"Shelby White," began Lucy. "You are a beautiful, fit woman who is in the prime of her life. Just enjoy it and quit worrying."

"Are you sure?"

I think we all rolled our eyes that time. "Go ask that guy next to us. He'll tell you the truth." I pointed over to the man lying on the lounge chair with a hat over his face to block out the sun about ten yards away. I then gave Shelby a look that said I wasn't joking. She stood up brushing the sand off of her clothes, and gave her long hair a flip over her shoulder. Pushing her shoulders back she walked over to the guy and posed by his head with her head cocked to the side.

"Excuse me sir." At his lack of a response, she cleared her throat loudly. "Sir, would you mind if I asked you a question?" It was at that moment that a gust of wind blew his hat off his face and Shelby let out a terrible scream.

Long story short, he was dead, as in doornail dead, can't beat a dead horse dead. "Well that answers our question," I said as I looked down at him while waiting for the police.

"What question is that," inquired Vana.

"Whether the guy in the closet was dead or playing dead. He was most definitely dead." For this was in fact, the same guy that fell out of the closet.

"How do you suppose they got him here without anyone seeing him?" asked Lucy.

"Weekend at Bernie's," stated Shelby matter of factly.

"What?" we all asked at the same time, looking at her.

"Don't you guys watch any movies? In Weekend at Bernie's two salesmen pretend their boss is still alive by carrying him around and pretending like he's just drunk. It was pretty funny."

"Serious question here," I said, clearing my throat. "Do we admit we saw the body at the house?" Lucy pursed her lips as she thought about it, while Vana chewed on her bottom lip. Shelby just scrunched up her face.

"There's no evidence to prove he was there." After a second, she added, "is there?" We all glanced at each other and then they all stared at me.

"What?" I asked.

"You're the sleuth," said Vana. "You tell us."

I didn't want to get in trouble for withholding evidence, but if there was no way to prove the body had been moved, why mention it? We already hadn't called the police to report the missing body in the first place. That thought right then clinched it.

"How do we report a missing body when we don't even know who it is? I say no." Vana, Lucy and Shelby all nodded quietly in agreement.

It was about this time that the police showed up and taped off the section of the beach. We gave our statements and let them know about the incident at the open house with the fake real estate agent and then they told us we could leave. By this time a large crowd had gathered around the area, curious as to what was going on.

We packed up our stuff and trudged back through the sand to the stairs going up to the house. As I climbed the stairs, I pulled out my phone and made a call. As I hung up, Vana asked, "was that Travis?"

I never could hide anything from her. "Yes. I thought maybe he might know someone out here that we could talk to."

"You mean help us out?" asked Lucy excitedly.

I sighed. "You're beginning to sound like Gloria."

"Well, she's a pretty dynamic woman."

I narrowed my eyes at her. "He said he might know someone and he'll have them get in touch with us.

Lucy looked at me with a big smile on her face. "We should hurry, Holly's got a big date tonight." Then she winked at me before entering the house.

PERFECT DATE

I met the girls after the date at the bar in a restaurant near the beach house. It was a cute beachy place with large windows overlooking the ocean called The Cove. It had a wrap-around outdoor seating area that we instantly fell in love with. A counter inside overlooked the ocean with a staircase to a second level. Lights on the outside of the restaurant illuminated the white froth on the waves in the dark. The girls were sitting by the large window, overlooking the water. They each had a fruity drink with an umbrella in it. I barely managed to get my butt in the seat before Lucy hit me up.

"So how was the date with Barry?" she asked, waggling her eyebrows for emphasis.

"It was the perfect date. He showed up wearing socks with his sandals and shorts." I said in a dreamy voice. "He's not a person to let weather dictate his fashion choices, his words. He ordered steak tartare and then nearly gagged when he saw it was practically raw. Trust me, I gagged too. Not to be outdone, he smothered it in a mixture of ketchup and steak sauce. You should have seen the waiter's face when he was asked for ketchup. After rushing to the bathroom to puke, I know because he came back and explained it to me in detail, he downed two beers and left me with the check because, and I quote, "I'm a working girl so I can afford it.""

Lucy clasped her hands over her face, looking horrified. After a few sputters she finally gasped in a tiny voice, "That was a perfect date?"

"A perfect date from hell. "You're not allowed to pick my dates anymore." Vana could hardly contain her laughter and finally fell over in the booth laughing till tears ran down her cheeks.

"Do you want a drink?" asked Shelby, sipping her pink concoction. The umbrella was tucked into a chunk of pineapple. "These are really good."

I shook my head. "No, one of us needs to remain level headed."

The girls frowned at me. "Why's that?" asked Vana.

I looked at each one in turn. "Now who's not watching the movies? The murderer always attacks when the victims are drunk. It's Murder Mystery 101."

"Do you really think someone is going to attack us?" whispered Shelby.

I shrugged my shoulders. "Better safe than sorry." Maybe it was the horrible date or the body on the beach, but I was feeling edgy, like someone was watching us. "Why was the dead guy in the closet, why was he moved and who was that woman? What's in that house that someone wants?"

Vana stabbed at the ice in her drink with the umbrella toothpick. "That's an interesting question. A woman dies from cancer, that's gonna cost a lot of money and the property taxes on that house must be a fortune every year. Where did she get her money from?

"I can pull up the property profile for the house," offered Lucy. "It won't tell us about her income, but we can find out when and how much she paid for it. I know some lenders who might be able to get me some more information."

"Is that legal?" asked Shelby.

"You'd be surprised just how much information you can get from public records," replied Lucy. "What did you say her name was?"

"Velma DiAngelo." A loud crash accompanied Vana's response as the server behind us dropped a tray of drinks. We all turned around at the sudden noise.

"I'm so sorry," said the server, a petite blonde girl wearing a black dress shirt and black jeans with a white apron. "I must have tripped. I didn't get any on you did I?" she asked worriedly as she tried to mop up the mess. We all grabbed some napkins and helped her to clean it up. "You don't need to help," she protested.

"That's quite all right," said Shelby as she put the glasses back on the tray. "Sometimes things happen."

"Are you okay?" inquired Lucy with a concerned look.

The waitress stood up with the tray and gathered all the damp napkins from us with a quick smile. "My name is Tiffany and I just started here. My first job actually. Thank you ladies. Are you here on vacation?"

"Yes, just for a few days," I said. "We're escaping from the snow. My name's Holly, and this is Lucy, Vana and Shelby." I indicated each one of them in turn.

"I hope you enjoy your stay and thank you again. If you need anything, let me know." She smiled again and backed away, turning just in time to avoid another table.

"That girl better grow some eyes in the back of her head or she's not going to make it as a waitress," remarked Shelby. Thankfully it was out of Tiffany's hearing.

I leaned back in my seat with my arms crossed over my chest. The girls looked back at me puzzled. Finally Lucy said, "what?"

"I thought we weren't getting involved in any sleuthing on this trip? Yet here you all are making sleuthing plans."

My phone buzzed and I pulled it out to see that it was a local area code.

I answered in my usual cheery voice. "Hello, Holly Holcraft. How may I help you?"

A deep male voice answered my response. "Hello Holly, my name is Carter Atley. Travis mentioned I might be of help to you?"

"Yes, could you hold on just one moment please?" I motioned to the girls to join me and we went into the ladies restroom. Shelby walked through the bathroom looking under each stall as she went. "What are you doing?" I hissed at her.

"Checking that it's empty."

Rolling my eyes, I clicked the speaker button on my phone. "Carter, I'm here with my friends and you're on speaker." After filling him in on the details, we waited for his response.

"Hmm, well ladies, you know as an officer I can't involve you in the investigation. I do owe Travis a favor though so I'll request to be put on the case so I can keep an eye on you just in case there's any trouble."

Lucy mouthed, "he sounds cute." I shushed her by narrowing my eyes at her and she mimed zipping her lips closed. "Any help you can give would be awesome," I said.

"Yes," added Shelby. "It was so frightening. You don't think they'll come after us do you?" She winked at me as she said it and I groaned inside.

"I would like to say no, but since we don't know who's behind it, it's probably better to be safe. Stay together and don't go anywhere alone. Can we meet up tomorrow so I can get an official statement?"

"We can go to the station if that's easier," said Shelby.

"Why don't we meet here at The Cove," I interjected quickly. There was no way, I was letting hormone crazy Shelby anywhere near a bunch of men in uniform. "How does 10 a.m. sound?"

"I'll see you then," said Carter before disconnecting.

Shelby smacked me on the shoulder. "Why did you say that? I was looking forward to going to the station."

"And that's why she did it," said Lucy and Vana together. What Shelby really needed was a date but we had all given up on that ages ago. Shelby held certain opinions that weren't necessarily appreciated by the male species. Somewhere out there was the right one for her but we were no longer assisting her in finding him.

"I think we need to get back into that house." My comment was met with silence.

"Hey you coming out of there anytime soon?" yelled a voice from the other side of the door.

"Yeah! Sorry!" Shelby yelled back as she flushed the toilet and then ran the sink water before grabbing some towels and bunching them up and throwing them in the trash.

'What are you, some kind of spy?" I asked her.

"What? It makes people feel better if they don't think you were just hogging up the bathroom for no good reason."

Lucy reached out and felt Shelby's forehead. "Nope, no fever."

Shelby brushed her hand out of the way and opened the bathroom door. "Sorry again, female issues." The woman just nodded in sympathy and let us go by. We made our way out to the car and began the drive back to the beach house. It had been a long day and I looked forward to relaxing in my pjs in bed.

Vana was driving. She always drove so we didn't have to listen to her driving advice. "Maybe we should drive by the house and check it out tonight," she suggested.

"No!" we all yelled in unison.

"I'm tired and going to sleep as soon as we get back," I said.

"Ditto," agreed Shelby and Lucy.

"Fine," Vana muttered.

"Why don't you call the agent in the morning and see if you can get more information about the woman that died. Maybe we can go back to see the house again in the morning," I suggested. Vana just nodded without taking her eyes from the road.

Shortly after arriving back at the house, we all retired to our rooms and went to sleep listening to the pounding of the surf.

AUDREY

"We can? Really? That's great. We'll see you at 8." Vana could hardly contain her excitement as she disconnected the call. We were all in the kitchen in our jammies getting coffee when Vana's phone had rung. "Audrey wants to talk to us and will let us in at eight so we need to hurry. It had been a surprise to receive a call from the agent this morning but I'm never one to look a gift horse in the mouth.

We all dressed quickly into our best clothes and then grabbed some muffins and coffee from the kitchen. "Shelby, you sure you want to come this morning?" asked Lucy as she stuffed a piece of banana nut muffin in her mouth.

Shelby twisted her lips and then nodded her head. "Yeah, I'm good." We finished our coffee on the patio without speaking. Saturday had dawned gray and overcast and fortunately, no breeze. Seagulls and tiny brown birds with long beaks, were searching the damp shore for crabs. We cleared our things away so they wouldn't attract the seagulls and then hopped in the car. Shelby lingered behind us to finish her muffin.

Audrey's car was in the driveway as we pulled in next to it. She opened the door as we reached it and greeted us warmly. "I'm so glad you could come." Audrey greeted us with a beautiful smile and put us instantly at ease. Some women are just like that, warm and inviting is their personality. She looked to be in her sixties and wore a floral print dress with sensible shoes.

"Um, if you don't mind," said Vana, "Could we see your ID please?"

"Oh, of course, of course. I would expect nothing less after all that dreadfulness." She pulled her wallet out of her bag and showed us her ID and gave us each a business card. "Velma was a dear friend of mine. I miss her terribly."

Her words touched a place in my heart that was still raw from thinking I'd lost my friend Betty to cancer. She was in a better place now, here on earth that is, not dead. It's funny how you can meet someone and then feel like you've known them your whole life. Audrey was that way. She reached out and grabbed our hands and led us to the couch in the living room.

"If I can be frank with you, I kind of need your help with something," she said as we settled ourselves. "I don't think, I mean, I'm not sure where to begin."

Vana, sitting next to her, reached out and touched her arm, "It's okay, just start at the beginning and tell us everything, including why we can't snoop in the cupboards." I raised my eyebrows at her. "What? I need to know, it's part of my nature."

Audrey laughed. "Oh, it's quite alright. I've already snooped in all of them. That was Charlie's rule. Velma's ex. He's a real piece of work."

"Oh, I understand," said Shelby, nodding. Her ex was a real piece of work too. I jumped into the conversation to avoid Shelby taking it over as that could be a long and unwieldy conversation.

"You said you wanted our help?"

Audrey's face took on a grim look. "Yes. Charlie was a snake and I think he did something to Velma."

"Why would you think that?" Lucy asked.

"Because of the way she died."

"From cancer?" I asked, confused.

"Yes. She'd never been sick a day in her life and then, just as soon as she divorces Charlie, she gets cancer and dies? I don't believe it."

Vana gave her a comforting hug. "She died from cancer, you can't fake cancer."

Audrey pushed herself away from Vana and started pacing the small room. "Really? People do it all the time. She went to an oncologist that Charlie referred her to, Harold Zimmerman. I think they were poisoning her. I never trusted him and that new wife of his. Her poor son, Velma just adored him." She stood there looking down at her hands.

"What exactly," I began hesitantly as I could understand not wanting to believe the worst. "Do you want us to help you with?"

Audrey let out a deep breath. "You seem like nice ladies. I want you to help me prove that she was poisoned." She looked at us expectantly as we exchanged glances and nods amongst each other.

"Great. Now, that's settled. Can we poke around in the cupboards?" Vana asked hopefully.

"You'll do it? Of course. Charlie never comes in here anyway. I think he wants to look for her will."

"Her will?" we all echoed. I seriously considered saying 'jinx' but figured now was not the time for it.

"A couple months ago, she became really despondent. She gave up a child when she was a teen and recently began a search but there were no results. At least, not that I know of. It's so sad really. She had no family left."

"Sorry if this is an indelicate question," said Vana, "but where did she get her money from? I mean, this isn't a cheap area to live in."

"It's quite alright. She had family money. Her parents were older and had done very well for themselves. Between that and insurance from work, she was very comfortable."

"Okay, I'm confused," I said. "How are you selling the house if there's no will?"

"This is why I want your help," she said. "I think she began to suspect towards the end that something was wrong. She put the house in a trust last month and insisted it be sold. She didn't want any risk of Charlie getting his hands on it. The money will be put into the trust until the will is found."

"Are you sure there is a will?" I asked.

Audrey nodded her head, "She said she had one. We had tea together and she told me she'd made a new one." Audrey sat back down and began to cry. Vana put her arm around Audrey's shoulders until she composed herself, then we searched the house from top to bottom and found zilch, nada. If there was a will, it wasn't here. Or someone else had already retrieved it. Either way, we couldn't know.

Sitting back in the car. Lucy spoke first. "Let's address the elephant in the room. We're only going to be here for two more days and it's the weekend. What can we do?"

"Maybe Holly could ask Harold on a date," giggled Shelby.

"We can find out where the oncologist lives and go door knocking," suggested Vana, ignoring Shelby's comment. "Plus there's this fantastic open house on Bayshore drive."

"Well," I drew out the word. "It's not the worst suggestion. "But first, we have to meet with Carter."

Lucy turned her lips down. "Doorknocking or the open house? Is the house as fantastic as the one we just left?" She turned her frown toward Vana.

Vana turned her head toward the side window and scratched behind her ear before answering. "That was just an introductory open house and it was the cheapest. The rest are better I swear." She punched the button to start the car and then glanced in the review mirror where she met Lucy's glaring eyes.

"Hey, the dead body wasn't my fault. It was just an added attraction," she protested.

"Do you hear yourself?" I asked. Instead of answering, she put the car in drive and headed for the restaurant.

CARTER

Carter Atley turned out to be a handsome detective about my age. Six foot five, sandy blonde hair with golden brown eyes. His t-shirt was sculpted to his body and tucked into his tight jeans. I think all our hearts beat a little faster when we saw him. We introduced each other and then gave him our statements.

"So you never actually saw anyone else?" he asked, focused on writing down notes in a notepad.

"No," said Lucy. "There was no one else there."

"Shelby, you didn't see anyone come outside or drive by?" Shelby shook her head 'no.' "I was too freaked out."

"Great," he said as he closed his notepad and put his pen away. "I think you ladies are safe enough as long as you stay together and stay away from the house. It looks like maybe they were looking for something in the house. Probably best if you just hang out at the beach." His condescending words ruffled my feathers.

"Even though there was a dead body at the beach?" demanded Shelby. She was right.

"You got me there," he said, grimacing. "That's not a normal thing here, I assure you." He handed me his card. "Give me a call if anything comes up or you remember anything else."

"Sure thing. I'll walk you out," I said as Shelby kicked me under the table. "Shelby, why don't you walk him out?"

"That's not...," he began, then apparently read the room. "Sure." Shelby turned back and winked at me as they walked toward the door.

"It's hard to believe such a horrible thing could occur in such a beautiful place," I sighed.

"Forget all that," jumped in Vana. "If we leave now, we can just make this open house on Bayshore Drive and then go doorknocking."

"That's a nice location," said Tiffany as we all jumped at her voice. She was the same one that had dropped the tray the night before. For a waitress, she was a bit too quiet. "Houses there are in the millions with awesome views and floor to ceiling windows."

Lucy frowned and tipped her head at Vana. "How much did you pay her to say that?" Vana's eyes opened wide in innocence before Tiffany spoke again.

"I'm sorry. She didn't pay me. It's just that I was driving around the city when I first arrived here and that place really sticks out." Vana gave Lucy a smug look.

"Well, thanks Tiffany, that makes me feel better," added Lucy. "Vana's last open house wasn't so great." She leaned over and whispered, "it had a dead body in it."

Tiffany's face went white. "A what?" she gasped. "There wasn't anything in the paper."

"No, no, no," I waved my hands back and forth. "It was some guy. They ended up finding his body on the beach."

"I'm confused," she said, although she didn't need to because her face conveyed everything. I explained what happened as best I could.

"How long have you been here?" I asked, to change the subject to more pleasant things.

"Only a month. I came to see my mom." For some reason she looked sad when she said it. "It's been a long time."

"Well I hope you have a nice visit," I said. Sometimes it's hard to be around family. My own mom is a bit of a handful and I haven't seen my sister...well it's been a long time too.

"I hope so too. I wanted to get a job first and show her that I can take care of myself."I tried calling yesterday but she's not answering her phone."

"Did she know you were coming?" I asked.

Tiffany nodded in affirmation, "just not exactly when."

I gave her a mom smile. "Maybe she's just been busy. I'm sure she'll call you back."

Shelby bounced back into the restaurant and Tiffany left to handle another customer.

"I've got a date," she singsonged to us. "We're going to the movies tonight to see Casablanca."

We all frowned at her. "Mm, he doesn't seem like that kinda guy," said Lucy, echoing what we were all thinking.

Shelby lifted her eyebrows, "Surprised me too but I love that old movie so we have to be done by 5 o'clock so I can get ready."

"Alright, let's get going then," said Vana picking up her keys and purse.

BAYSHORE DRIVE

The next open house was absolutely amazing. It was everything Lucy had wanted and more. Vana was a schmuck for holding out on us and making us go to that other house yesterday. Especially because it literally came with a skeleton in the closet.

Vana was right about millionaires today because everyone we saw was in jeans and a nice top, some wore suit jackets, like us, over their clothes. We walked through the bright airy space in awe. Sure, we had million dollar homes in Appleby, but it was a mountain community with log cabins and dark wood. This place was amazing, bright and airy.

We took a moment to admire the view from the third floor balcony overlooking the ocean. The sun had come out and seagulls wheeled through the air calling out to their friends on the ground. "Hey," Vana tapped my arm. "Isn't that the real estate agent from the other house?" She pointed to the beach below us where we could just see the top of the fake agent's blonde head. She was talking to another person we couldn't see because they were standing directly under the balcony.

I squinted my eyes in that direction, "Who do you think she's talking to and what is she doing here?"

"That would be Mrs. DiAngelo, and she was looking at purchasing this property," said a deep male voice next to us.

My heart jumped into my throat as I spun around. I really needed to become more aware of my surroundings. "She, she wants to buy?" I finally stammered out.

"Hi, I'm Joe Estevez, the agent for this property." An elegant man in his thirties dressed in a tailored dark gray suit with a red tie and pocket handkerchief, held out his hand for me to shake, which I did. He had a nice warm, firm handshake which made me think he was an honest man. He peered down at the woman. "Goldie has been here several times to see the place, but I don't believe she's a real estate agent."

Goldie, well now we had a name for her. "I must be mistaken," I said smiling. "This is a beautiful home. I'm an agent myself." I handed him my business card because, yes, I do take them on vacation with me. "We're just visiting but sometimes, we do get referrals to other locations. Can I get your card?"

"Sure thing," he said, reaching into his jacket pocket for one. "Goldie said she's coming into an inheritance soon and wants this property but like I told her, it's first come, first serve. I can't hang onto a property on a promise."

"I totally understand, Joe. I've had to say that same thing myself before," I nodded in sympathy thinking of Jacob Martin back in Appleby. For some reason he was fixated on a house that had been sold and he had just been too slow and missed out. Now he was angry about it. "Would you let me know if she does make an offer on it? I'm curious to see how the buyers operate in this area compared to the actual price."

"I wouldn't normally, but seeing as we're not competition, sure," he said with a warm smile. "And maybe you can use me as a referral if you get any clients out this way?"

"Thank you, Joe. I definitely will." I smiled to myself all the way back to the car. Would he actually let me know? Maybe, maybe not, but the potential for a future client is a strong lure in the real estate world.

I waited until we were all back in the car and driving to Harold's house before I asked the question that was driving me crazy. "Did you see who she was talking to?"

The girls all shook their heads. "Whoever it was never came into view," said Lucy despondently. "Do you think it was whoever killed that guy?"

I twisted my lips. She could have been talking to anyone. She had been too far away to hear anything. It could even have been her son. I shook my head and shrugged.

A CLUE

Harold Zimmerman lived in an upscale neighborhood in the suburbs above the city. I was a little surprised it wasn't closer to the beach but I guess not everybody wants to live with all the tourists. The neighborhood wasn't gated, which was a plus for us. We parked down the street from his house and with our business cards in hand, because we never go anywhere without them, Vana and I approached his house. We left Shelby and Lucy to watch the car because it seemed like four women might be a bit intimidating.

We didn't really have a game plan other than winging it. Harold's house was a single story surrounded by flower beds that the weeds were beginning to invade. Two small steps led up to a covered front porch surrounded by a flowering hedge. "Somebody really likes flowers here," commented Vana as we mounted the two steps to the front door.

A short, dignified looking man answered our knock dressed in a blue patterned sweater and beige slacks. "Hello, so sorry to disturb you but we're real estate agents, I'm Vana and this is Holly, and we have a buyer looking to purchase in this neighborhood. We just wanted to know how happy you are living here and if you have any issues with crime." We both smiled at him.

He opened his mouth to speak when a rather large Airedale terrier barreled through the door, smacked into me and knocked me off the porch. Fortunately, the bushes lining the walkway broke my fall but left me with my arms and legs askew in the air.

Alarmed, the man hurried down the steps and extended his hand to help me up. "I am so sorry. You must forgive Siegfried. He is rather boisterous." He had a delightful German accent.

Vana was failing badly at trying to hide her laughter as she tried to console me. "Oh Holly, are you okay?"

"Yes, thank you for your concern," I glared in her direction as I brushed off my clothes. "And thank you Mr?"

"Harold Zimmerman," he said as he corralled the ever exuberant Sigfried.

Harold indicated his front door. "Please come in and get cleaned up." I hesitated but Vana grabbed my arm and hustled me inside.

"Thank you Mr. Zimmerman, we really appreciate it," she said.

"No problem at all and call me Harold. The bathroom is down the hall, first door on the right." As I made my way into the bathroom, I could hear Vana talking to Harold about his house. My first glance into the mirror showed me Harold was right to direct me to the bathroom. My hair was filled with twigs and leaves, and there was a smudge of yuck across my left cheek. My clothes hardly fared better with dirt streaks and detritus all over. After cleaning out my hair and brushing off my clothes, the floor was now filthy. How could I leave the poor man's bath like this? I grabbed some tissues and did my best to clean up the mess. After surveying the floor one final time and brushing the rest under the rug, literally, I felt I had done a decent job. Maybe he had a housekeeper.

I came back out to the living room feeling much better. "Thank you for your courtesy Harold," said Vana, ushering me to the door. "We really must get going, so many houses to see today. Goodbye, Siegfried. He really is a cute dog." The dog in question was sitting on the floor brushing it with his tail.

Vana hustled me along to the car and hopped in the driver's seat. She didn't speak until we were well away from the house. "It's not him.

He stopped practicing two years ago leaving the practice in the capable hands of his assistant."

"So what do we do now?" I asked, twisting in the back seat. Soreness was beginning to settle in my shoulders and hips.

Vana held up her forefinger to stop me. "He left his practice to Goldie Bergren. A blonde, slightly overweight woman who looks like a real estate agent."

Annoyance rose up in me. "You really need to stop doing that. Next time just tell us the important info right at the start."

"Hey, sometimes that's the only fun I get," she retorted.

"Ladies, hellooo," said Shelby sitting next to me, "what are we going to do?"

"Why don't we ask Vana if she has any more relevant information first," I said sugary sweetly.

"Okay, fine. You take all the fun out of it. Harold's first wife died of cancer and that's why he went into that field. Goldie is a family friend of his and of Velma's ex-husband. There was a group picture of them on the wall on a fishing boat. Sadly, no proof of anything nefarious."

"Great. At least we remove him as a suspect. What do we know about the ex-husband? Shelby, can you do your social media magic and look him up?"

"It's too bad we don't know the adoptive baby's name," sighed Lucy from the front seat.

"You don't suspect them do you?" questioned Shelby. "What is that smell?" We all sniffed and then rolled down the windows as the odor of dog poop permeated the air. "Everybody check your shoes."

"Well it can't be us," said Lucy, "Neither one of us got out of the car."

"Not me," I said, thankful for once that the problem wasn't mine.

"Pulling over," said Vana, although it was easier said than done as we were now on the busy highway with no shoulder so we had to content ourselves with hanging our heads out the windows. Vana finally pulled into a gas station and then spent the next ten minutes cleaning off her shoe, the carpet and the gas and brake pedals.

"Still not as funny as watching you fly through the air," giggled Shelby as she fiddled with her phone.

"Did you record me?" I asked, shocked.

"Maybe."

"Find anything about the ex yet?" cut in Lucy quickly.

"Yes, actually. I found a picture of them with the son." Shelby turned her phone around and we looked at a picture of Goldie standing next to a distinguished looking older man with graying hair. A teenager was next to the woman and a little off to the side as if he didn't want to be in the picture. They were standing next to a boat named Velma.

"Goldie is the new wife?" I clarified. "I guess this explains why she was impersonating the agent and how she knew to steal Audrey's car."

"Looks like he still had feelings for his ex-wife. He never changed the name of the boat anyway," observed Lucy lounging against the side of the car. No one was willing to sit inside right now. "Hmm, maybe the gas station sells air fresheners?"

Vana glared at her from her position on the floor, half in and half out of the car. "Maybe, wanna go take a look?"

Lucy pushed off from the car door and headed to the store. "Does anybody want anything else?"

"Gum," said Shelby.

"Diet coke," I called after her. "So Vana, after you get done cleaning maybe we could go check out the marina?"

With a great oomph, Vana staggered to her feet. "It gets harder every time to get off the ground. Ugh. The marina sounds like a good idea."

I knew exactly how she felt, especially since I seemed to be getting more sore by the minute. "Are you sure this is how you want to spend your weekend?"

"This is the most exciting thing I've done in a long time," stated Shelby. "I'm game."

Vana scoffed. "You ran out at the first sign of a dead body."

Shelby shrugged, "I'm over it now. I think."

Lucy returned from the convenience store. "Here ladies," she said, handing out the requested items. "Vana, Febreeze for you and maybe we can drive with the windows down for a bit. That dog sure made some pungent droppings. I got you a Snickers, so you don't get hangry after all that cleaning."

"Good thinking," said Vana, taking the proffered treat.

"I'm starving and I don't want a candy bar," said Shelby. "Let's go back to that restaurant and get some lunch."

"Sounds good to me," I said.

CONFRONTATION

We found a booth overlooking the beach and admired the waves while we waited for the waitress to take our drink order. We all ordered the salmon with rice as it wasn't what we usually got in the mountains, especially in the winter. And it was delicious. The fish was cooked to perfection and the white wine added a pleasant additional taste. I love when you get that combination flavor like coffee and donuts.

The waitress, an older woman with her dark hair done up in a loose bun on top of her head, brought over a glass of wine and whispered in my ear, "courtesy of the man at the bar."

Without even looking in that direction, I replied, "no."

"What?" she asked, surprised.

So I replied a little louder, "I said no. I don't accept drinks from strangers and I've already had a glass with my lunch."

"Oh, the designated driver." She nodded in a knowing manner.

"No. I'm just not drinking anymore because I don't want to. And please don't bring any more drinks that we haven't specifically ordered. Thank you very much," I looked at her name tag, "Rhonda," I finished with a big smile on my face.

"Sure, thing honey," she replied then walked back to the bar. This time I did watch the middle-aged man with the slight beer belly at the bar as she brought the drink back, refused. He did not take it well. His face got red and I could make out that he was yelling at her.

"Making friends everywhere we go," muttered Shelby into her glass of wine.

"Seriously Shelby, you're the one who was all 'women first' the last time we were in a bar," I pointed out.

"But it was free," she whined. "I would've drunk it."

Lucy compressed her lips together and shook her head. "What kind of message would that be? You can't have it both ways. You either stand up for women's rights all the time or you don't. Don't send mixed messages."

"Shelby what is with you lately? You're all over the place. Is everything okay?" I asked, concerned.

She glanced at Vana before responding. It was really quick but I caught it. Vana and I would be talking later. "I think it's the menopause," she responded, then buried her face in her glass. I accepted her answer knowing I was going to get the real answer later.

Not too long later, we got up to leave and headed to the door. The man from the bar was standing in our way.

"You think you're better than me? Huh? I was just giving you a free drink. Is there something wrong with that?" He snarled. I was so done with these drunk, belligerent men who thought you owed them something just because they bought you a drink you didn't ask for. Their parents really should have taught them better.

"Look sir, it's early afternoon. It's way too early for you to be this angry already," I said.

At that moment he pulled a knife from his pocket and before I even had a chance to respond, Shelby had kicked the knife from his hand and flipped him over her onto his back, then grabbed his wrist and forced him onto his belly where she proceeded to kneel on his back still holding his wrist.

"Mmm, Shelby? Is there something you need to tell us?" I asked, shocked. What is it with my friends knowing Kung Fu moves? She looked up, her brown hair hanging over her flushed face.

"Um, I've been taking karate classes? Thought I told you guys."

"No, no you didn't. Pretty sure I would have remembered that," cut in Vana.

After the police came and arrested the man, the bartender approached us, a tall good-looking guy with dark hair. "Ladies, are you okay?"

We all nodded in affirmation. "Great. Listen, if you ever have a problem again, just use the code word 'sunshine' at the bar. We'll take care of it from there."

"Gotcha," said Shelby as she snapped her fingers and winked at him.

Vana grabbed her arm and pulled her out of the restaurant. "Thank you for the information, we'll be sure to do that," she called back to him as she hustled Shelby out to the car. "Thanks a lot Shelbs. I love that place. Don't mess it up for us."

"What? I just saved you from a mad man," she protested.

Lucy rolled her eyes. "Yes, thank you, but next time let's let the staff handle it."

They all looked at me for back up but I just shrugged my shoulders. "She did handle it and that guy was way out of line."

"He was drunk," Vana retorted.

"Exactly, you never know how a drunk guy is going to respond. One of you could have gotten hurt," Shelby retorted back.

"So what do we do now?" I asked. "We didn't even discuss the case."

"Let's head back to the house," suggested Lucy. "The balcony is the perfect place to discuss things. Oh, and I spoke to my friend. She said we could use it for another few days if we want." Lucy looked around at each of us as Vana blipped the car open.

"Sounds good to me," I said and then yelled, "shotgun," as I hopped in the front seat.

CONTEMPLATION

The view on the beach house balcony was fantastic. Seagulls swooped down and tried to steal the lunches from the beach goers who left their items unattended. I marveled at how large of a bag a seagull could carry. One landed on our balcony and I looked over and then smacked a chip out of Shelby's hand.

"What? I just wanted to see it up close."

"Heck no. You give one a chip and then pretty soon, they're all up here. There's a reason they have 'no feeding the birds' signs all around," Lucy berated her.

Vana cleared her throat. "Ahem. Where are we with our clues?"

"Nowhere," sighed Shelby. "I thought this was going to be more exciting." She crossed her arms on the table and laid her head down on them.

Lucy picked up the tale. "One," she ticked off the numbers on her fingers as she went. "Dead guy on the beach, unknown. Two, Harold Zimmerman appears to be innocent. Three, Goldie, his partner, faked being a real estate agent and now runs the practice. Meaning, she could be the one that possibly poisoned Velma."

Vana interrupted her synopsis. "Speaking of poison. I heard that chemo medication is pretty bad stuff. If they told her she had cancer but she didn't, it could really kill her."

"That's right," said Shelby. "People die from their cancer treatments all the time."

"That's so sad," said Lucy. "The thing they think is going to save them, is the one that actually kills them."

"Remember, it does save a lot of people's lives too. But you're right Vana and now we have means and motive. Poisoned by chemo and for her money," I said.

"The son didn't look too excited about them being together. Maybe he's someone we should talk to," mused Lucy.

"That's a great idea," I said. "It's the weekend, maybe we should check out Charlie's boat? I'd be hanging out there if I was a teenager."

"Sounds good," said Lucy. "Why don't we split up? Shelby and I can go check out the local park and you and Vana can check out the boat."

"Wait. We only have one car," said Vana.

"That's the best part," said Lucy. "The park is just a mile down the beach. They have an area for exercise and stuff like that. Kind of like on Venice beach."

"Are you sure you want to take Shelby there?" I asked.

"Oh yeah, she'll be perfect."

"Hey, I'm sitting right here," she protested.

"Yes, you are," said Lucy. "Now let's go get on some shorts and running shoes." She jumped up and disappeared into the house as she said it. She really enjoyed going to the gym and staying fit. Exercising on the beach was right up her alley.

Shelby looked at each of us in turn and then at the open door. "I just want you to know, I am not running. She wasn't serious about that was she? Lucy? We're not really running right?" Her voice rose with each word. She went inside with a worried look on her face and Vana and I began laughing.

"We should probably get going," said Vana. "Who knows how long it takes teenagers to get bored."

"What if they took the boat out?"

Vana shrugged, "I guess we wait around for a while and see if they come back."

With plans made, Shelby and Lucy set off down the beach and Vana and I hopped in the car for a quick trip to the harbor which turned out to be packed with boats, mostly covered for the winter. Seagulls were keeping watch on the light poles and there were a couple of sea lions on the walkways between the parked boats.

We were in luck and the boat, well really it was a yacht, was parked at the end of a pier tucked in between two other fancy boats that were covered up for the winter. Beyond the boats, the dock was empty on both sides.

Did I mention the sea lions? We had just turned down another dock when a series of loud barks pierced the air behind us. Vana and I both jumped at the sound and spun around. The biggest sea lion I have ever seen was charging at us. Panicked, we jumped over the boat railing next to us and onto the boat docked there, where we watched the raging sea lion bob its head back and forth at us, our hearts pounding in our chests.

A quiet click behind us made us freeze. "Hands up ladies," said a quiet voice.

"Turn around slowly," instructed the voice again and that's exactly what we did, with our hands in the air. We found ourselves face to face with a shotgun held by Ahab from Moby Dick. The only thing he needed was a peg leg. A fishing cap was pulled down low over his eyes, he had a mustache with a full beard, and a pipe hung out of the corner of his mouth. I side eyed Vana to see if she was seeing the same thing I was.

"Sorry sir," she apologized. "We just jumped over because of the sea lion. We'll just be going now."

"Aye, ye might want to wait on that a bit. Ole Bob gets a bit cranky in the afternoon." He set the gun down and walked over to a bucket on the deck where he pulled out a couple fish. "Sorry if I scared you, but we've been getting people wanting to take Instagram photos on the boat." He shook his head sadly. "People these days have no regard for others' personal property."

He tossed the two fish to Bob, who gobbled them both up and dived over the side of the pier into the water. "Um, thank you?" I said hesitantly. "We were actually just looking for the *Velma*. My name is Holly and this is my friend Vana."

"Well you found her." He narrowed his eyes at us suspiciously.

"We were actually looking for Velma's step-son and thought maybe he would be here?" Vana ended the sentence in a question.

"The poor kid's not here. What business did you have with him?"

Deciding that anyone who feeds the sea lions had to be a good guy, I decided to confide in him. "A friend of Velma's asked if we would help her look into Velma's death. She's suspicious of Velma's husband."

"Are you two detectives?"

"Vana and I glanced at each other before answering. "We're real estate agents," we said at the same time. Ahab's eyebrows rose at the answer. He paused to consider our response before answering.

"Seeing as you're not working for Mr. DiAngelo, I'll tell you what I know. I don't like that man. Velma hired me to take care of the boat but the mister always complained about me, said I didn't give off the right aesthetic, if you know what I mean." He winked at us before continuing.

"They got divorced and she took sick. Poor Velma, she never got well again," he said, shaking his head sadly. I could see her death affected him deeply. "She was the best thing that ever happened to that boy. I was suspicious of it myself seeing as how Mr. DiAngelo never grieved a day for her. But that boy Nick, he was all torn to pieces. He tried to hide it, but I could see."

"Thank you, Mr..." I prompted him.

"Name's not important," he said. "Anything else I can help you with?"

"Velma's friend said she had a diary?"

"Aye, that she did. She wrote in it most days. Might be that Nick knows something about it. He didn't like his stepdad or mom very much." He looked up and down the pier. "You two should probably get going, I wouldn't want anyone else getting hurt."

"Thank you, sir," I said as he helped Vana and I back over the railing and onto the pier. "Just one more thing."

"What would that be?"

"Do you think Goldie and Charlie were having an affair before he got divorced?" That would definitely be a motive for murder.

"I'd think anything of that man. He fired me once Velma was too sick to come out on the boat anymore.." Ahab spit into the water. "Goodbye ladies."

We hadn't really gotten any answers but at least he did confirm that there was a diary and perhaps that's what the house had been ransacked for. We still didn't know who the dead body was though and what could be in the diary that was so important? Was Velma killed because of the diary? The more I thought about it, the more convinced I was that she had been murdered.

"Hold up Vana, I just need to catch a fish," I said as we reached the main pier and then pulled my phone out of my purse. Focused on my phone I realized something was amiss at her silence and looked up. Vana was staring at me with pursed lips. "What are you doing?" she asked.

"I promised Chloe that I would catch her a fish," I said as if that explained everything.

"With a phone."

"Yeah. You don't play Pokemon?"

"Aren't you a little old for that game?"

"I just do it so I can give Chloe things. She really loves it." Chloe is my four-year-old granddaughter and I love playing games with her. So if she wants a fish, I'm gonna get her a fish.

"Are you playing Pokemon?" asked a male voice. I looked up to see Carter standing there dressed in a graphic tee with tiny fish swimming around fat trees. My heart beat a little faster.

"Yes. Do you play?"

"I dabble in it from time to time," he replied. I flashed a triumphant look at Vana.

"I wanted to catch my granddaughter a fish but I'm out of Poke balls," I added with a frown.

"Hey no problem, I'll send you a gift. That'll give you at least one, if you're any good."

I flashed him a smile. "Oh, I'm good." Vana groaned. "Oh, look, there's a tower here." I spun the medallion and collected my balls and caught the fish for Chloe on my first try and pumped my fist in the air. "Thank you. She'll be so excited." I put my phone back in my bag. "So what brings you down here? Are you investigating a criminal?"

He looked so cute in his beach shorts and t-shirt. The wind was blowing his hair around his face and I found myself wanting to run my fingers through it. Shelby was going to be jealous she missed him.

"Naw, even us detectives get a day off now and then. I just like to come down here and enjoy the weather. What about you ladies?"

Vana spoke up first before I could respond. "We're just enjoying the weather too. We don't get to see this often where we're from."

Carter looked at her a moment and then nodded his head, "It is pretty nice down here. Too bad you have to leave tomorrow."

"Oh, we're not," said Vana, staring back at him. "We're going to stay for another couple days." Laughing, she added with a shrug, "who knows when we'll be back out here. Did you find out who the dead guy was?"

"Dead guy? Uh, no. Not yet. Did you ladies come up with anything?"

"Uh, uh. We're on vacation. We'll leave the sleuthing up to you," she said. I gave her a frowny look until Carter turned around to face me and I quickly changed it into a smile. What was she up to?

We said our goodbyes. "Stay out of trouble," he said as he waved to us, then we hurried back to our car.

Vana sat in the driver's seat but she didn't start the car. "Do you find it funny that he was in the same place as us?"

"No. I mean, yeah, maybe. What about it?"

"I felt like he was fishing for information. Maybe he's not a good detective. You should call Travis and ask him about him."

"Hmm, are we really staying longer?"

Vana gave me a long look. "Do you think we can wrap this up in another day?"

"Okay. Maybe Shelby and Lucy had better luck. Let's call them," I suggested. Vana started the car and called them over the car's bluetooth as she drove. She was getting the touch screen down like she'd been doing it all her life.

"Hey, Lucy, we're heading your way. No luck here. Did you find out anything?" she asked.

"Vana, yeah. Nick's here, there's just a little problem."

BIG BLUE OCEAN

M ere moments later we pulled into the parking lot for the park. It was located mere steps away from the beach which made it convenient for parents of kids who didn't want to swim. I couldn't see Shelby or Lucy in the park area, although there were tons of parents with young children playing on the swings and monkey bars. I let my eyes roam over towards the beach and found the two of them waving their arms at us. We took off our shoes and struggled through the sand until we got to them standing near the water. It was much easier to walk on the packed sand near the water's edge. Out in the ocean, several surfers were hanging out waiting for the perfect wave.

"Okay, we're here. Where's Nick?"

Lucy grimaced and looked at Shelby who tilted her head at the ocean. "He's out there waiting for a wave. If we want to talk to him, we're gonna have to go to him. He hasn't shown any indication of catching a wave. I think he looks depressed."

"How do you know that?" I asked. Nick was pretty far out and although I could see a kid on a board, I certainly couldn't see his face. Shelby reached into her bag and pulled out her binoculars. "Oh." I looked over at Vana who immediately responded with, "oh no way. I'm not going out there, you're the sleuther." Lucy and Shelby were suddenly interested in a shell on the beach.

"Fine, I'll do it," I said and walked over to a couple guys in their twenties in black wet suits, standing on the beach with their surfboards in hand. "Mind if I borrow your surfboard? The girls bet me that I couldn't catch a wave and I want to prove them wrong."

The tall lean guy on the left gave me the once over from my head to my toes, then nodded at me. "Sure, I'll let you give it a try." I had a feeling he really agreed so he could get a funny video out of it. I looked but didn't see any phones on them, not even a gopro. After a quick briefing on the basics, I grabbed the board and headed off into the surf.

After the initial shock, the water actually felt warmer once I was fully immersed. Getting over the little waves was not too difficult but it took me two tries to time it right to get over the big wave, but I did it. It was gorgeous out here. Seagulls flew overhead amongst the white fluffy clouds in the blue sky. It was quite a difference from the freezing cold and overcast sky we had left back in Appleby. Several other surfers were sitting on surfboards waiting to catch a wave but I found Nick right away because he had a lost look on his face, his shoulders slumped. I felt like he wasn't waiting for a wave as much as just waiting. I sat up on the board with my feet dangling in the water and let the current push me closer to him.

He was wearing a wetsuit and I wished I had one on as, out of the water, the breeze made it chillier. I waved at him. "Hi, I'm Holly. Any tips for a first time surfer?"

He bit his bottom lip, reluctant to speak and looked at me doubtfully. "Hang on. You probably won't get up the first time, but that's okay." He seemed to relax a little bit while he was talking.

I gave him my best mom smile. "You seem a little stressed, I thought surfing was supposed to be relaxing."

This time he laughed. "You're right. Sometimes, I just get so caught up in my thoughts I forget."

"That's okay, it happens to all of us." I suddenly decided to just go with the truth. I took a deep breath and let it out, then said, "your name is Nick right? I saw a picture of you at Dr. Zimmerman's house." He tensed up a bit at my comment. "Look, I'm not going to lie to you, I came out here to talk to you. My friends and I are helping Audrey look into Velma's death. Audrey thinks that maybe she was poisoned. Would you know anything that could help us?" I gave him my most innocent, endearing look.

At the mention of Velma's name, his eyes watered and I almost thought he would catch the big wave heading our way but he didn't. Instead he sighed deeply and answered me in a quiet voice. "I really miss her. She was the best mom to me." He paused again to think. "Since you're helping Audrey, you must be a friend. I think my mom was cheating with Charlie while Velma was sick. How awful do you have to be to do something like that? She was such a nice lady, she was teaching me how to play the guitar. My mom thought it was stupid." His voice caught on a sob and we sat there in silence listening to the gulls and the other surfers calling to each other as we gently bobbed on the water, waiting for him to compose himself.

"Hey Nick, you gonna catch this wave?" yelled one of them. Nick shook his head and waved at the other guy to go for it.

"What do you need to know?" he finally asked me.

"Somebody broke into her house and we think they were looking for her diary. Audrey said Velma was searching for the baby she gave up for adoption twenty years ago and maybe that information is in there. Nick looked back at the shore as if he was searching for someone. "Did she ever mention that to you?"

He suddenly stiffened and said quietly "paddle to the crest of the wave and then pull your knees up onto the board. Let's go." Then he added, "bob."

I copied his movements and then moved my head up and down and back and forth. Nick looked back at me, his eyes wide before screaming, "no! Bob!"

I frowned and then realized he was looking past me. I turned and started paddling like mad. The crazy sea lion from the dock was heading our way fast and he looked angry. Somehow I managed to catch the crest of the wave and managed to pull my knees up under my chest. Just as I was congratulating myself on my achievement, everything went sideways and I was tumbled head over heels under the water.

Fear gripped me as the waves tumbled me around. The harness on the board pulled against my ankle. There was no way to tell which way was up and I panicked until I realized the board tugging on me was probably floating and I let it carry me to the surface where I gasped for air.

The wave finally dumped me unceremoniously face down on the sand and added insult to injury by dumpling a large pile of seaweed on my head. Did I mention I hate seaweed? I picked up my head enough to see the girls' shoes walking towards me through my dripping hair. One of them reached down and pulled the seaweed off me.

"Thank you," I mumbled into the sand where I lay exhausted.

"Are you okay lady?" asked the guy whose board I had borrowed just before he screamed. "What did you do to my board?"

"Hey man, that's pretty cool," said his friend. "How many people get a sea lion bite on their boards?"

"Oh, ya ya, it's just awesome." The sarcasm came through clearly. "That board was super expensive."

"It's okay," I mumbled, lifting my head up again, which I shouldn't have because I could see the girls struggling not to laugh. "I'll pay for it. It's my fault Bob bit it. I didn't paddle fast enough."

"Here," I heard Vana say. "It's Holly's business card. Just send the bill here." I heard the two guys discussing the issue as they walked away, one complaining and one consoling.

"Bob? Really Holly, you need to stop naming these animals," Lucy chided me.

"I didn't name it," I said defensively as I sat all the way up. Sand covered the entire front of my body. "Nick was giving me instructions and he said bob so I started moving my head up and down. I didn't know he meant the sea lion." I looked around for him, but the snarky sea lion was nowhere to be found. I flopped onto my back on the sand and stared up at the sky and my friends who had their lips pressed tightly together. A giggle escaped from Shelby's lips. "Can I just die now?" I whined.

Shelby was losing the laughter battle and so Vana sent her to the car to get a towel from the trunk of the car. I wonder what else she has hidden in that trunk. "Where's Nick?" I asked suddenly, sitting up and looking around.

Wherever he had gone, he was now nowhere in sight and I could hardly blame him after I had confronted him like that. A person should be safe in the middle of the ocean. I could see Shelby coming back across the sand. "What did you find out?" Lucy asked me.

"He said he thinks his mom, fake Audrey, and Charlie were having an affair. That's all I really got because Bob interrupted us."

"He is pretty mean," confirmed Vana.

Shelby finally reached us and dropped the towel on my lap. "You guys won't believe what I just saw. Nick and his mom were at the showers and she was totally chewing him out. I feel so sorry for him."

"Did they see you?" I asked, concerned as Goldie may have killed someone.

Shelby shrugged, "it doesn't matter. I don't think she ever saw me at the house. Anyway, she told Nick to stay away from us in a loud threatening manner. She wanted to know what he said to you but he said 'nothing.'"

"So just what do we do now? We have to leave tomorrow and I have a date soon." Shelby waggled her eyebrows at me.

Maybe we should stay later. We were already scheduled to fly out on the red eye and that still gave us the whole day tomorrow. Would that be enough time? Shelby could cancel the date but then she wouldn't be able to pump Carter for information. Ugh. There's never enough time in the day. I used the towel to dry most of myself and get the sand off my clothes. I wouldn't be truly dry until I could change clothes.

"Let's get dinner," said Shelby.

Lucy looked at her, confusion written across her face. "Aren't you going on a date?"

Shelby took a deep breath and let it out. "It's to the movies and just popcorn. I don't want to be focused on my stomach when I need to concentrate on answers. How come he hasn't called or anything?"

"Food sounds good," said Vana. "Maybe he's waiting to see you tonight? Besides, he's probably really busy right now. A dead body on the beach probably has all of the cops busy right now."

"He's probably investigating," I said. "We ran into him at the pier when we were looking for the *Velma*. Vana and I filled in Lucy and Shelby on our narrow escape as we walked back to the car. It really was just a short trip back to the beach house and I put my window down all the way to enjoy the fresh air. It was beautiful. A cool breeze came off the water and the sun made diamonds on the waves. As we passed the location where the body was, I could see one lonely cop keeping watch over the crime scene, the tape still marking off the area.

I shivered at the thought that it happened so close to our beach house. Could it have been a coincidence or was it a warning? How would anyone have known where we were staying? "Ladies, you don't suppose someone put that body there deliberately, do you?"

They all frowned as they thought about it. "You think maybe someone followed us from the open house?" asked Shelby. She looked scared.

"Maybe you shouldn't go out tonight," I said, concerned.

She shook her head and smiled. "I'm probably over thinking things and I'll be out with a police detective. I'm sure I'll be totally safe." We all smiled back at her but I could tell they were unnerved by the thought. We pulled into the driveway, Vana checking twice that the car was locked. Lucy jiggled the door handle before she opened it just to make sure it was still locked and then locked it again after we entered.

I took a long hot shower and then dressed in a long sleeved shirt and jeans. I would grab my jacket from the hook by the door on my way out. It was winter after all and evening came pretty quick now. I came into the living room to find the other girls similarly attired. Shelby beat me to the front passenger seat and stood there looking at it with a frown on her face. I glanced in as I walked by.

"Oops, sorry," I said at the sand covering it. "Do you want me to sit there?"

"No. I've got it." She returned to the house and came back moments later with a small broom and swept off the seat. She put the broom by the front door and returned to the car.

At the restaurant, the hostess seated us by the window where we could see the sun beginning to set. The sky was just beginning to turn a pale pink at the edges.

"I saw what you did," Tiffany stated as she placed menus in front of us."That was awesome. Where do I learn something like that?" It took me a second to place what she was talking about.

Placing her elbow on the table, Shelby put her chin on her hand and leaned forward conspiratorially. "Karate. That and self-defense classes. You can't go wrong with those. Plus all those guys in uniform," she added winking. "If you know what I mean."

"Karate uniform or police uniform?" Tiffany asked, puzzled.

"Don't listen to her," said Vana as she perused the menu. "Her hormones are out of whack. I think I'll have the Dover sole please." I opted for the clam chowder, as did Lucy, and Shelby settled for grilled chicken salad.

After Tiffany left to put our orders in, we all looked at each other. Lucy spoke first. "I think we need to find out who that dead body was. There was nothing in the paper this morning but maybe if I call the paper, someone will talk to me."

We paused when Tiffany brought us glasses of water and then Lucy piped up with a suggestion I didn't want. "Maybe we should go back to the boat."

I raised my eyebrows, whether in shock or surprise, I wasn't sure. "What for? Do you want to meet Bob personally? Or get shot?"

"Ahab doesn't sound like he likes them very much. Perhaps he would just look the other way," suggested Lucy. Something she said triggered a memory in my brain but it was gone just as quickly.

We were once again interrupted by Tiffany bringing our food. The smells from the dishes were tantalizing and my tummy rumbled in anticipation. As Tiffany set the dishes down she asked, "Are you guys here on vacation?"

"Mmhmm," said Vana, already tucking into her meal. She placed her hand over her mouth as she continued to chew. "This food is awesome." Tiffany's face beamed.

Lucy picked up her spoon and sampled her chowder. "Oh, wow. This is fantastic."

I could see Shelby was beginning to regret her choice. "Would you like to switch?" I offered.

"No, but maybe just one little taste?" she asked hopefully.

"Sure." I pushed my bowl over closer to her. "Yes, we are here on vacation. Just for the weekend. We're leaving tomorrow night," I said, finally answering Tiffany's question.

"You know there are other places to eat around here. You don't have to come here every time. But I agree, the food is excellent," she said with a smile, then left to help her other customers.

"I really like that girl," said Shelby, helping herself to another spoonful of my chowder. I sat there regretting my decision to let her taste it. I turned around at a tap on my shoulder to see Tiffany holding another bowl of chowder which she set in front of me.

She indicated Shelby with her chin. "I knew you would need it after she tasted it."

I laughed. "Thanks. And I'm never letting her taste my food again." I directed a glare at Shelby who didn't even notice.

"I'll bring you a box for the salad," she said and went back to work.

The next few minutes were spent enjoying our meal. Vana finally sat back and wiped her lips with a napkin. "There may be other restaurants but I think I'll keep eating here."

Tiffany brought us a box and the bill. "Tiffany, were you able to reach your mom?" asked Vana as she reached for the check. Tiffany shook her head 'no.' "I went by the house but she wasn't there."

"And she didn't call back?" I asked in shock. What kind of a mother doesn't return a phone call.

Tiffany looked sheepish. "I didn't leave a message."

"How do you expect to get a call back if you don't leave a message?" admonished Shelby, bluntly as usual. "You need to call her back and leave a message. I actually block phone numbers that I don't know. There's so much spam going around now."

Tiffany looked a little worried now. "Oh no, I don't want her to block me. Do you think she blocked me?" Her voice rose as she spoke.

"Shelby," I hissed at her. "Stop it." And then to Tiffany, "I'm sure it'll be fine. If you're still getting her voice mail then she hasn't blocked you. Just be sure you leave a message the next time you call." Tiffany grabbed Vana's card and the check and left to go process the bill.

"Way to go Shelby," said Lucy, elbowing her in the shoulder. "Freak the poor girl out, why don't you?"

Shelby wet her lips with her tongue. "I'm just saying, if you're going to go to all the trouble to make a phone call, you should leave a message. Does she just expect her mom to have ESP?"

"She's not wrong," I said. Tiffany brought Vana's card and receipt back. "Thanks Tiff. If you don't mind me asking, what's your mom's name?"

Tiffany smiled. "Not at all. It's Ellen. Isn't that pretty?"

"It certainly is," said Vana. She tucked her receipt into her purse and we made our way out to the parking lot. I'm pretty sure that receipt is going to be a tax deduction at the end of the year.

"It's only five. We could drive over to the marina and check out the boat and get back in time for Shelby's movie," said Lucy. "You could text Carter that you'll meet him there."

"That's it!" I shouted out. The girls looked at me like I was crazy. "Ahab said he got fired. What was he doing on the *Velma*?"

"You think he was looking for the diary?" asked Lucy.

I could see Shelby considering the idea of prowling around a boat in the dark. "I'm in," she said. "I'll just text Carter that I'll meet him at the movies. Lucy gave a smug look, then we all climbed into the rental car for the short trip to the marina. It was a good thing it was almost fully dark now because four women sneaking around was going to be kind of conspicuous.

The marina in the evening is a beautiful sight. Lights from the stores and boats reflected off the glassy water. The sounds of the evening seemed to be muted by the water and, thankfully, the sea lions had gone off somewhere to sleep. Only a few people were out taking in the evening air but we could hear music from the nearby restaurants. All of the rest of the shops appeared to be closed for the night.

Vana led the way to *Velma's* slip. I swear that woman was born with GPS. Since the evening was so quiet, we were still quite a ways away when we began to hear angry voices coming from the vicinity of the boat. We crept closer until we could make out what they were saying.

"I don't want you anywhere near those women. They are leaving on Sunday so just stay home until they're gone," screamed a female voice.

"But mom," said a voice I recognized as Nick's. "It's the weekend, I've got plans with my friends."

"Well cancel them. I have plans tonight and you're going with me. It's not bad enough that you treated that woman as more of a mother than me. Don't think I didn't know what you were doing, going to her house all the time.

"But mom, it was just music lessons," protested Nick.

Don't say another word. End of discussion!" declared his mom with finality.

"How does she know when we're leaving?" hissed Lucy.

We all shushed her as footsteps came in our direction. We ducked down and ran down a perpendicular dock, praying they wouldn't see us in the dark. Something wet tickled the back of my leg and I clamped my hands over my mouth to muffle a scream of terror before I turned and saw a seal behind me. A second later and my heart nearly stopped at the sound of a man's voice.

"It's okay girls, she's gone back inside the boat and that's not Bob," said a familiar voice. I turned around to see Ahab standing at the entrance to the dock we were on. I looked back again at the seal. It really was kind of cute with a dark wet face and long whiskers. Ahab wiped his hands on his pants as we got to our feet warily. Glances around us showed there was just the one seal and it wasn't interested in us.

Ahab extended his hand. "Ladies. I'm sorry I haven't been forthright with you. My name is Patrick Flannigan. I saw you sneakin' 'round over here." I gulped. If he saw us, who else did? "Not to worry," he said. "No one else noticed ya. The witch is too self-involved to notice anythin' but herself."

I looked around the dock with trepidation. "Are you sure Bob isn't around?"

"Naw. He hangs around at the end of the dock by the *Velma*. Everyone pretty much leaves that space to him. The only one he really tolerated was Velma. She seemed to have a thing for him."

He paused and put his hand on his chin as if deciding his next move. I was proven right by his next words. "You help that kid and you and I are friends for life." He nodded his head as if the deal was done. We all stood in silence contemplating his words. The water made a gentle splashing sound as it lapped against the boats.

"Uh, okay," agreed Shelby, breaking the silence. "Thanks Mr. uh, Flannigan. But we're running out of clues."

"Why don't we step onto the boat and away from pryin' eyes," he said as he looked around. He led us to a large fishing boat at the end of the dock we were on. He helped us onto the boat and then into a small saloon under the deck.

"Is that an Irish lilt I detect in your voice?" asked Shelby, always the flirt, although Patrick was her senior by decades.

Patrick gave a broad smile, showing his teeth. "Aye, that it 'tis." The room we were in had a table and chairs fixed to the floor and a small kitchen and sink set in the side.

Because of his kindness, I spoke before thinking. "Patrick, if your boat is over here. What were you doing by the *Velma*?" Immediately, I regretted my words. He seemed like a nice guy, but what if he wasn't. What if he was up to no good?

He grimaced. "You got me. I was up to no good." I tried not to express my shock. Could he read my mind? "I was looking for the diary when you showed up." At our grimace, he stammered, "no, no, not for my own benefit. It was for Nick. Velma had mentioned she was looking for her kid and I think maybe it's Nick. They spent so much time together. Why would she do that if he wasn't her kid? Although, if she can make friends with that cranky seal, she can make friends with just about anyone. I know he wants to go to college and the money would help him do that. Anything to get him away from that she-devil."

The relief on our faces was palpable. "Do you know if Nick was adopted?" I asked

"No, but people don't always tell their kids the truth," he stated then shook his head. "I didn't tell him my suspicions. I wouldn't do that. I do think the truth is in the diary but I've no idea where it could be."

Poor guy, he looked so miserable. I could really believe that he was only looking out for Nick and I was really relieved that I could call him Patrick now instead of Ahab. It was quiet on the boat and the gentle rocking was beginning to make me sleepy. A large yawn cracked my jaws, which reminded me I had places to be before I could go to bed.

"Patrick, I'm assuming you searched the boat for the diary."

Patrick compressed his lips in a frown. "Aye, I did, and nothing.

We were interrupted by my phone ringing. The caller ID showed a local number. "Hello, Holly speaking." A whispered voice came over the other end. "Holly? This is Nick. Can I meet you?"

I made arrangements to meet him back at the restaurant so we could drop off Shelby on the way. At this point I wanted as few people as possible to know where we were staying.

"Well Patrick, what can you tell us?" I asked as I returned my phone to my purse.

WE DROPPED OFF SHELBY a block from the cinema and we dropped Lucy off at a library that would be open late, then drove on to the restaurant where we asked for a secluded booth. Patrick really hadn't anything to tell us beyond what he'd already said. He seemed like a down to earth guy who was just trying to make a living. Tiffany seated us outside in a corner of the patio. "You were working this morning. Don't you get a break?" I asked her as she seated us.

"Another waitress called in sick, so I'm covering for her, but I have tomorrow off," she said with a smile.

"We're waiting for someone. If you could bring him back here that would be great," said Vana. We described Nick to her and she said she would be discreet.

"Alright, so Harold is a nice guy. His assistant Goldie is a gold digger, a cheater and a terrible mom. Nick is just a poor kid and Velma was his guardian angel." I summed up what we knew so far when a thought struck me. "Where's Charlie?"

It being Saturday, many places weren't open but Lucy knew someone in town who would let her use their computer and so she went to track down his address. Meanwhile Vana and I searched on our phones for any more information about Charlie or Goldie.

"Too bad we didn't get a picture of the dead guy," I said.

Vana looked at me like I was crazy. "What on earth would you want that for?"

"So we could do an image search of his face."

"Oh. I guess that would be a good idea. Let me text Shelby, maybe she can get one from Carter."

"Good idea. Where do you suppose Charlie could be?" I flicked through the social media posts on Goldie's page, pausing at one of the pictures. "Hey, look at this. Do you think he's in construction?"

Vana leaned over to look at the picture that showed Charlie wearing a tool belt. "Very probably. I don't think people generally have a full tool belt if they aren't in the building profession. What do the comments say?"

I scrolled down the list of comments. "Looks like he was helping build tiny houses for the homeless. The comments all seem pretty positive towards him. From these comments it doesn't seem like he's such a bad guy."

Vana sat back and shook her head. "Maybe he just got caught up with the wrong woman. It wouldn't be the first time a guy went bad for a girl. I was looking at Velma's social media. Audrey was right, from the time she got diagnosed until she died, was only nine months. She looks totally healthy in all of her photos until she started treatment. Isn't that weird?" She set her phone down in front of me so I could see the photos.

"I don't know. I hear chemo can be really tough sometimes. I just wish we had more answers." I chewed on my thumb nail, thinking. "If the house is being sold and left in the trust, how much money is left to fight over?"

"Maybe Charlie doesn't know about the trust. Audrey doesn't strike me as someone who would just volunteer that information."

"Two million dollars makes for a good motive."

Tiffany made her way across the floor toward us with Nick in tow. He kept glancing nervously around the restaurant. As he got to the table he ducked into the booth next to me and kept his head down, his dark hair falling over his eyes. "I can't let my mom see me. She'll kill me." I got the sense he was only half kidding about that.

"What was it you wanted to see us for?" I asked gently.

"It's just, what you were asking me about on the surfboard," he paused.

"Yeah, when you almost got eaten by a seal," cut in Vana. At this comment, Nick cracked a smile.

"That was pretty funny," he said. "Velma did have a kid. She said she was just a little older than me. She looked so sad when she said it. I think she was looking for her, and made me promise not to tell anyone about it. But I can trust you right? If you're helping Audrey, and Patrick says you're good people." He fiddled with the napkin on the table. His face was scrunched in thought, as if he was trying to make a decision.

He began, "Her diary..." when his phone rang. "It's my mom, she has a tracker on my phone. I should go." He jumped up from the table and hurried across the restaurant. At the door he paused to speak to Tiffany. He used one hand to brush the hair out of his face and they could see a smile on his face.

"I think that boy just found himself a girl," mused Vana. "Good for him."

As I turned to look, I saw something disturbing. "Oh, oh, his mom is coming in. Quick, let's go." I grabbed Vana and we dashed to the women's restroom, where we hid in the bathroom stalls like we were teenagers.

I giggled. "I haven't done this in a long while."

"If I didn't feel so sorry for Nick, I wouldn't be doing it now," retorted Vana. Her phone rang and I heard her rummage for a minute before answering it.

"It's Lucy," she whispered. "What did you learn? Because we're hiding in the bathroom from Nick's mom. Okay." A second later, Lucy's voice came from the speaker.

"Charlie has a house an hour away from here, close to the desert. I called the number but no one answered. I looked up the pictures online and it's nothing special. Probably not worth more than four or five hundred thousand. The money from Velma's house would definitely buy an upgrade. I'm texting you my address, come pick me up."

Vana's phone dinged and she clicked on the map app. "Got it. We'll be there in ten minutes."

We left the stalls and washed our hands. You never know who touched it last. Peeking out the bathroom door, we saw no sign of Nick and so we made our way to the restaurant entrance, while cautiously looking around.

"It's okay, they drove away already. You're safe," said Tiffany from behind us. I'm sorry to say, we both jumped at her voice. "He seems like a really nice kid," she added. "I gave him my number."

"I hope that works out for you," I said.

"Just watch out for his mom," Vana added.

We stepped outside to find a light rain was falling. Hustling to the car, we jumped in and drove to our rendezvous with Lucy.

As we pulled to a stop at a red light, I saw a man with a homeless sign standing in the rain. "It's pretty sad that we can't find homes for all these people in such a prosperous state," Vana said sadly as the light turned green.

"Wait," I called out as we continued on the road. "Stop here." We were in front of a CVS. Vana parked while I ran inside, purchased an umbrella and came back out and jumped in the back seat behind her.

"I know it's raining, but I have an umbrella in the car," Vana protested. "I thought you were going to be less frivolous with your spending?" Vana had been on my case about my budgeting since last year. I'd been struggling financially, mostly due to the shenanigans of Bonnie Belmar, a fellow real estate agent who was sabotaging my career, and Vana had decided that she was going to get me back on track. It was hard though, not spending money on things I didn't really need but made me feel good to buy. But that poor bum in the rain really did need an umbrella and it was the right thing to do.

"Turn around and go back to that intersection," I said instead of giving her an explanation. As we approached the intersection and the red light, she slowed the car.

"Get in the left turn lane," I ordered and she complied with a question mark written on her face until she saw him.

"Uh huh, I see."

Rolling the window down, I handed him the umbrella. "Bless you," he said and I responded the same. Putting the window back up, I leaned back against the seat and looked up to see Vana watching me in the mirror.

"He'd better use that," she remarked.

"You'd better go turn already," I said as the car behind us honked its horn. Vana stepped on the gas and wham! A car jumped the light and collided with the passenger side of our car. I thanked the Lord I wasn't sitting there.

Now the horns were really blaring. Vana limped the car out of the traffic, listening to the passenger tire rub against the fender wall all the way to the side of the road. We both got out to survey the damage and the homeless guy courteously came over and held the umbrella over our heads. I gave Vana a smug look.

"You got the rental insurance right?" I asked.

"Yeah, I'll call them now," she added, punching in the number. The police showed up shortly after and then a tow truck followed to haul off the cars as the other guy's car wasn't going anywhere either.

The rental company was awesome and dropped off another car for us to use while Vana and I both looked at the 2024 MINI Cooper in dismay. Sure it was cute and it was new but it was so tiny.

"Um, I guess you are gonna have to sit in the backseat when we pick up Shelby," commented Vana wryly.

Don't get me wrong, I think Mini's are super cute and I wouldn't mind having one, but there really was no way Shelby would fit in the back seat. It was a hatchback, maybe we could stick her back there.

"Sorry," said the car tech as he handed me the keys. "It was all that was left. If you check back in later, someone may return a bigger car later."

I gave him a half hearted smile. "Great. Thanks."

By the time we picked up Lucy, we were an hour late. She busted out laughing as soon as she saw the car. "Maybe we can put Shelby in the trunk."

I had to say though, the car fit nicely in the drive, when we returned home.

With Shelby at the movies, the girls and I were getting bored at the house. "Look, I know the movie already started but why don't we go and watch it anyway?" I asked. With nothing better to do, they both agreed with me and we snuck in the back of the theater with a little less than half of the movie to go.

We snuck out as soon as the credits started appearing and I excused myself to the bathroom. Always the cautious type, especially during flu season, I used the paper towel from drying my hands to open the bathroom door a foot, then wedged my foot and arm in it to open it the rest of the way, throwing the used towel in the trash outside the door.

Lucy and Vana were waiting across the hall for me with Shelby. So much for being sneaky. A flash of silver caught my eye from the man on the right of Shelby and I heard a gunshot echo through the hall. I watched in awe as Shelby thrust her elbow up and into his neck as hard as she could and then did it again and again. I guess those karate classes were working after all! As he collapsed forward, She reached across with her left hand and grabbed his gun hand and then twisted it around and to his back until she was sitting on him and pulled the gun from his hand with her right hand.

Unless he wanted his arm broken, he wasn't going to move. He looked to be young, maybe even late teens. A woman's voice cut through the lobby screaming, "My son, my son, don't hurt him!" Looking around, I could see that everyone in the hall and the lobby was cowering on the floor. Seconds later, a large woman came hurrying around the hall. "My boy, he don't mean to hurt anyone." She kept talking and moving toward Shelby.

"Stop, lady. If you come any closer, I'll shoot you," She said in as stern of a voice as she could but the woman continued to come closer. "Stop her!" I yelled as loudly as I could. "Now!" Finally a couple men stepped in front of her to stop her from getting closer as she erupted into shrieks of hysterics.

The boy under Shelby began to cry silently but made no attempt to get up. Three guys finally had to tackle the woman to the floor as she continued to protest her son's innocence.

A short time later sirens filled the air and moments later, the police had arrived and cuffed both the son and the mom.

"Excuse me," I said as I approached the handcuffed mother. "Why did you do this?"

"I didn't do nothing," she spat at me. "My son is just confused."

"Really," I said. "Then why did you know it was your son before you even came around the corner and saw him?"

Silence met me. As she glared at me, her mouth was working but no words came out. "You put your son up to it didn't you? What? Was he supposed to die in a gunfight? Then you're the grieving mother? Was this all just to get sympathy? Who was he supposed to kill anyway?"

"She did it."

"Shut up, son!"

"No. You wanted me to die." yelled her son in shocked realization. "She wanted me to kill my dad's girlfriend. She lied to me and set me up." The words just spewed from his mouth revealing the whole sordid plot. "Keep her away from me!" he screamed as she suddenly lunged and broke free from the cops.

The next few moments did not go well for her before she was finally sitting in the back of the police car. Her son was loaded into an ambulance and silence settled over the theater.

Looking around I saw that most people had left and I caught a glimpse of Nick and his mom scurrying out the door, held open by an older gentlemen in a dark business suit. We all gave our statements to the police and then I realized someone was missing. "Where's Carter?"

"Um, he said something about checking in on the investigation," said Shelby. "He got a text while we were in the movie."

"Kinda weird, he wasn't here for this," commented Vana. "Him being a cop and all." Shelby shrugged.

"So how was the date?" asked Lucy.

Shelby looked a bit disappointed. "I didn't get any information from him. He actually seemed more interested in what we had been doing."

"Well, I have to say that was pretty impressive," I said.

"What? The shooting?"

"You, taking the gunman down."

Shelby shrugged, "Oh, that was just instinct. Don't mess with a momma."

"I need to start taking those karate classes with you," said Lucy and I caught a funny look on Shelby's face when she said it.

"I knew it," said a familiar voice and I turned around to see Travis standing there. "I knew if there was trouble somewhere, you would be near it." My heart was suddenly pounding in my chest and my knees felt weak.

I was dumbfounded. What was he doing here? "Can I take you home? I think they want to close the theater," he said. Looking around, I realized that we were the last ones there. I couldn't think. Travis, here? What, why? Not that I minded, or did I? This thinking was getting me nowhere. Was he here just to prevent me from pursuing this investigation? Which one of the girls called him in? And why did he come? Now I was getting angry. The girls had no right to get him to interfere, especially when they were so gung ho about pursuing the idea in the first place.

Getting ready to refuse the offer, Vana spoke up with the truth. "Probably a good idea, since Shelby's going to take up the whole backseat anyway."

"Say what?" asked Shelby and I could hear Vana explaining all about the car situation as they walked through the door.

"Well, I guess that just leaves me and you," said Travis. "You can update me on your investigation on the way."

The pounding in my heart had ceased but butterflies had now taken up residence in my belly. With the most innocent look on my face, I responded, "I have no idea what you're talking about."

Travis looked at me and laughed. "That's not what my friend says. I had to park at the back end of the lot, I'll go get the car and come back and get you." I watched him leave and then hurried to catch up to Lucy and Vana.

"Hey, isn't that the car that cut us off?" asked Shelby. I looked up to see a beige Mercedes just exiting at the far end of the parking lot. As another car drove past, the driver was illuminated by the headlights.

"I think that's the guy that was holding the door open for Goldie and her son earlier," I said. Had she moved on to another husband?

He could have just been being polite, but there was something in the way he had looked at her, almost as if he was escorting her out like you would if you had been on a date. The thought continued to pester me.

"They were here?" asked Vana.

"Yeah. I saw them as they were leaving the theatre," I said. Looking around the lot, I saw there were only a handful left besides ours, they were probably employee cars. The outlier was a red Mercedes. I wondered if it belonged to the woman that had been arrested.

Shelby saw where I was looking. "See, now that's what I'm talking about. Red. Beautiful."

A shadowy figure was leaning against the mini and as we approached the figure peeled itself away from the car and approached us. I grabbed Shelby's arm to stop her and Vana from going any closer. The figure turned out to be Carter with a sheepish grin on his face. "Sorry, about leaving you like that." He seemed a little nervous.

"Uh, Shelby, could I talk to you for a minute? In private?" Shelby glanced at us and we nodded back.

"Yeah, sure." They walked about fifty feet away from us. If they hoped to be private, they were out of luck. The still night air carried every word back to us. Vana and I turned away from them and pretended not to listen but of course we were listening. Vana tucked her hair behind her ear so she could hear better.

Carter ran his hand through his dark hair then tucked his thumbs in the belt loops on his pants. "That was pretty incredible," he said.

"The shooting?" asked Shelby.

"You, taking the gunman down."

"Oh, that was instinct, don't mess with a momma," said Shelby flippantly.

"Hey, yeah, so don't take this the wrong way, but I don't think this is going to work out." There was a hesitation before he began speaking again. I turned my head to get a better look but Vana grabbed my arm and turned me back.

"Don't look," she hissed at me.

"But you were just looking," I protested.

"I'm better at it. Shhh."

Carter continued on and we missed the first few words "...I mean I just can't compete with that. Would you really have shot her?"

"Let me get this straight." Uh oh. This was about to go very badly for Carter. I glanced around the lot wondering what was taking Travis so long. "You don't want to date me because I defended myself?"

"No. I mean, I see you don't understand."

"Why don't you explain it to me," she said sweetly. Shelby had started tapping her foot. That was always a bad sign.

Carter looked down at the ground before answering. Not that I was looking or anything. "It's just that it's kind of emasculating, you know? I mean it's probably going to be on the news and how is it going to look for me? My girl took down a gunman. I'll never live it down. I mean the guys are going to rag on me endlessly. You have no idea how vicious they can be."

Vana and I both grimaced and started walking away from them. "Uh, I think I see Travis's car coming," I said looking at his headlights which were taking way too long to get to me.

"Oh no you don't," said Vana as she grabbed my arm to hold me back. "If Shelby's going to kill him, we are both going to be witnesses.

"Oh no I do get it. Thank you for saving me from you because I don't date misogynistic chauvinists. I hope you find the helpless girl you're looking for." Shelby's voice kept gaining strength with each word until she was nearly shouting. I couldn't help it and glanced behind to see what horror Shelby was committing, but she wasn't. Instead she was walking toward us, anger etched on her face.

Now I wanted to hear what she had to say so of course that was when Travis pulled up. Reluctantly I said goodnight and climbed into the passenger seat of Travis's car. My heart went pitter pat looking at his handsome profile which then made me nervous and I started blabbering.

"Look Travis, the girls had no right to call you out here. They are the ones that encouraged this investigation." I opened my eyes wide. "I actually wanted to have nothing to do with it."

"Okay, we'll go with that," he said. "But the girls didn't call me, my cousin did."

"Your cousin?"

"Yes, Rey, she asked for my help. She didn't say anything about you needing help."

"Oh. Well, okay then. It's nice to see you."

"It's nice to see you too," he laughed. "Now about that investigation you were going to fill me in on?" I spent the short ride to the beach house filling him in on our recent events. It's not like he could do anything about it anyway as it's not his jurisdiction. I was a little puzzled by his attitude. It was almost like he was *encouraging* me to investigate.

I couldn't ask any questions though because all too soon we were back at the house saying our goodbye's and he drove off to spend the night at his cousin's house. Well, there's always tomorrow.

EARLY THE NEXT MORNING I woke up to a silent house. Padding into the kitchen in my robe. Through the kitchen window, I could see two seagulls perched on the balcony railing. I made a pot of coffee and then stood on the balcony enjoying the warm winter sun. It was surprising how warm it was without the sun out.

I sipped my coffee and enjoyed the sound of the waves crashing on the shore. It was different from the silence of snow but they were both calming in their own ways. I would miss it when we left tonight.

Lucy came out to join me moments later still in her pajamas, her hands cupped around a steaming cup of coffee. "Nice morning huh." Her voice was raspy from sleeping.

"Yup." We both stood for several moments in silence, just listening to the nature surrounding us. "I need some more coffee," I said finally. "Are Vana and Shelby still sleeping?"

"I think Vana's in the bathroom and Shelby must be sleeping. Lucy was acting funny. "What?" I asked.

"Good thing you weren't on a date with Travis's friend last night."

I looked at her puzzled. "Why would I be on a date with Carter?"

"Why wouldn't you?"

I threw my hands up in exasperation. "Are you going somewhere with this?"

"I guess the question should be, why weren't you interested?" She peered at me over the rim of her coffee cup. Would it have been terrible if I had been on a date when Travis showed up unexpectedly? Carter was attractive and had a job. Had I felt disappointed when Shelby jumped at him? I didn't think so. Why was that?

"You looked pretty happy to see Travis last night," suggested Lucy. If I was being honest with myself, I would have to agree with her. Fortunately, I didn't have to answer because my phone rang. "Travis, hi," I answered.

"Hi," he said and my heart did a flip flop as his deep voice filled the air. Lucy snatched the phone from my hand.

"Travis, you should come over for breakfast, Vana's cooking." She winked at me with a smile as she said it. I let out an angry huff as I reached for the phone but missed as she danced out of my reach.

"I'd love that. Mind if I bring my cousin?"

"Your cousin?" she asked, puzzled.

"Yeah, Rey, I stayed at her house last night. Holly didn't tell you?"

I lifted my shoulders and made a face, "oops?"

"Hey, Why don't you invite Carter too?" Shelby would probably enjoy having her hunk over for breakfast.

"Who's Carter?" At the words, a sudden queasiness began in my belly. Unlike the butterflies, this feeling wasn't pleasant and put me on edge.

"Carter Atley, with the local police. He said you referred him to us. He said you were friends." We looked at each other with wide frightened eyes as we waited for his response.

"Carter? I don't know any Carter," said Travis. "Audrey is my cousin. I thought since you were both real estate agents, maybe she could help you out."

"Help me out with what?" I snapped, now angry. "I needed police help, not real estate help!"

Travis let out a big breath over the phone. "She has contacts." When his response was met with silence he added, "is Carter the guy that Shelby went out with last night?" He lied to us in the restaurant. Somebody had killed that man at the open house and then carried the body to the beach. Lucy had said it had to be a man that moved the body. Was Carter the man?

I barely registered the words when Travis said, "Audrey and I will be there in 15 minutes. Don't go anywhere," then disconnected the call.

"I think we need to talk to Shelby and see what she found out," I said, walking down the hall to her room.

Vana met us in the hallway. Of course she was fully dressed. "She's not here. She got a call late and must have gone out again."

"Without telling us?" I asked. The queasiness began working its way up my spine.

"Why? What's wrong?"

"Tell her Lucy, I'm going to call Shelby." Making my way back to the living room, I checked for any messages from Shelby. Nada. After dialing her number, the phone went straight to voicemail. "Hey Shelbs, it's Holly, time to rise and shine. We got things to do today, so get back here." I disconnected and then sent the same message in a quick text. It's always best to have every base covered.

The girls were in the kitchen when I walked back out. "Phone went straight to voice mail. She must have it off, or it died." They both looked at me with scared looks and I probably reflected the same.

Where was Shelby?

While we dressed and then waited for Travis and Audrey to show up, we repeatedly called Shelby's phone but it went to voicemail every time.

A knock at the door sent us all into frantic mode until we heard Travis's voice call out. "It's me Travis, let me in."

I unlocked the front door and escorted them both into the room. Travis looked worried and Audrey looked frightened.

I was stunned. Audrey, the agent whose open house we went to is your cousin and the friend you recommended?"

"Didn't I mention that?" frowned Travis, apparently trying to recall his conversation.

"You called her Rey," I said. "Oh." I smacked my forehead with the palm of my hand. "Rey, short for Audrey. Who is Carter Atley?" He and Audrey exchanged concerned looks.

"What?" I asked. He knew something.

"I called the local police on the way here. The body on the beach was Charlie DiAngelo."

"Velma's husband?" I asked, shocked. No wonder we couldn't find him.

"We should all sit down." Vana was always practical. We all dispersed to the living room where the worry about Shelby kept everyone from enjoying the view.

I stood up to pace back and forth, my thoughts racing at a frantic pace. "Velma was possibly poisoned. Charlie was murdered and his body stuffed in a closet at the house and then moved to the beach. Who stands to gain from their deaths?"

"It had to be Carter who moved the body." Vana stated what the three of us were thinking. If it had been Carter, would he hurt Shelby?

Audrey took off her jacket and gloves and laid them on the couch before speaking. "Charlie and Goldie stood to gain from Velma's death. Only Goldie stands to gain from Charlie's death."

"Okay, so Goldie. Is Carter her new boyfriend? Did he move Charlie's body? And who killed Charlie and where? Has he been playing us this whole time? Travis?" If he knew who Charlie was, maybe he knew more. Frowning at him, I asked a different question instead.

"Travis, why are you here?"

My question threw him off and he just looked at me blankly. "What?"

"You are the first person to say we should stay out of police investigations and leave it to the professionals. So why are you here?"

He looked at me with a befuddled expression. He closed his eyes and looked down and Audrey, seated next to him, put her hand over his. His next words wouldn't have astounded me more than if Santa Claus came walking through the door. "I came to help you."

I narrowed my eyes at him suspiciously. "You knowingly were going to help me interfere with a police investigation?"

He twisted his lips around as if answering would kill him and then blurted out, "yes." To say I was shocked was the understatement of the year, perhaps even the decade. He reached over and put his hand on Audrey's and looked in her eyes for a moment. "Audrey made me realize how short life is. And, quite frankly, I'm getting old. I want to spend my old with you. I know you think you're not ready, but honey, you're old too. We should be old together."

I couldn't speak, trying as I was not to cry.

Travis suddenly stood and grabbed my hands. "Holly, I miss you. Audrey said you might be in danger and I came to help you myself. I am going to interfere in a police investigation for you."

The tears that had been threatening, proceeded to slip down my cheeks. "That was the most loving thing anyone has ever said to me," I finally managed to get out.

Vana cleared her throat. "We really need to find Shelby."

"Yes, yes we do," I said, wiping the tears from my cheeks. "Travis is going to help us now and Audrey is his friend, not Carter. Got it."

"And you're old, honey. Don't forget that part," cracked Lucy.

"Right, then. Where do we look first?" I asked.

"The boat," Vana and Lucy both said it together.

My phone pinged with a text message. "It's from Shelby," I said with a sigh of relief. Swiping up to open my screen, my heart plummeted.

"If you want to see Shelby again, go home."

Everyone had crowded around to read the message. "So what do we do now?" whispered Audrey anxiously. "I'm so sorry, I got you into this." Travis grabbed her shoulders and steered her back to the couch.

"Well, we're not going home." I caught Travis's eye and we smiled at each other.

"This is not the time to be happy," Vana chided us.

"We can work with this. This confirms that Carter has her and that means we can track him down. He's got to live somewhere. We'll find his house and what car he drives. I think you could be right about the boat. If he's working with Goldie, he could very well have stashed her on the boat. Lucy, can you purchase tickets for our return flight?"

"But you just said we're not leaving," she protested.

"I know, but it has to look real to him. I'm going to text back the flight details and tell him that he needs to bring Shelby to the airport or we're not getting on the plane."

Vana pumped her fist in the air. "Great! And then we can bust him."

I shook my head. "We don't have any evidence. We've got to find the diary and use it to get him to confess. "Goldie must think that she is going to inherit the money from Velma because Charlie is dead. She'll pay a lot of money for that diary."

Vana frowned, "We're going to blackmail her? I'm confused."

"No." I looked at Travis. "How do we make it look like we got on the plane?"

"Let me make some calls." He pulled his phone out of his pocket and walked down the hall. I watched until his backside disappeared into one of the rooms.

"What do you want me to do?" asked Audrey. "I'm so sorry. I should never have asked for your help."

Vana sat beside her and wrapped her arm around her shoulders and I sat down on the other side and did the same. "It's not your fault," I said. "You had no idea. You just wanted to help your friend and that's a wonderful thing."

"Besides," said Vana, indicating me, "it's what she does." She was right. It was what I do, or at least what I do now. Shelby was my friend, and I'm pretty sure could take care of herself. We just needed to find her before she hurt somebody.

"Done!" yelled Lucy. "Our flights are set to leave at noon." Travis walked back into the room, just in time to hear.

"I just talked to Scott Williams. Remember that big investigation he had recently?" I remembered that he had one, not what it was. It was just before he came to help out in Appleby. "It was in cooperation with the FBI. When I explained what happened, he offered to help. Some agents from the field office are going to take our place on the plane. We'll hide out until it takes off and then sneak away. Of course, this means they will be coordinating from here on out."

I texted Shelby's phone with the information and demanded she meet us there or we wouldn't board the plane.

"That still gives us a few hours to check out the boat." I gave him my best innocent look.

He let out a loud sigh. "We should check and see if anyone is watching the house first before we sneak out." I couldn't help myself. I squealed out loud and gave him a quick hug. I guess he really was here to help. Him being on my side was feeling pretty good. Not that I needed the help; but I did appreciate the help.

We put Shelby's binoculars to good use and used them to spy on the beach and road from several different vantage points. Travis finally admitted that he didn't think we were being watched. "I'm pretty sure no one's out there. If what you're saying is right, then it may just be Goldie and Carter."

"Did the coroner say how Charlie was killed?" I asked.

"Well, now that's a funny thing," said Travis. "It appears he died of a heart attack."

"What?! So he wasn't murdered?" exclaimed Vana. "Then why all the subterfuge?"

"Well he did have a head wound, but it didn't kill him," said Travis.

I turned away from the window overlooking the beach where I had been watching the people. "Maybe it has something to do with the will. Or maybe, they wanted the body away from the house." I shook my head. "We searched it pretty thoroughly. There's no way the diary is in there. Audrey, you searched it too right?"

We all looked her way at my question. She looked like a deer in the headlights for a second. "Yes, I did. And I didn't find anything."

"You know," said Lucy slowly, thinking as she was speaking. "I think sometimes people put a time limit in their will. You know, if your heir dies within such and such time after your death, they don't inherit and their share goes back to the estate."

"That could explain why they hid the body. But a good coroner can pinpoint the time of death unless the body was frozen. In this case, they determined Charlie died sometime Thursday morning."

Audrey sighed audibly. "The diary isn't in the house. Doesn't that mean someone must have it? I really wanted to find it and find the child. I mean, It would mean so much to know that a part of Velma lives on."

There was something about what Audrey said that bothered me. "The house was open when we got there but you didn't open it, because Goldie stole your car. She didn't open it because she pulled up after we got there. So who opened the house? Charlie? Carter? Who put today's paper in the dresser drawer?"

Vana's stomach growled loudly. "Mm, maybe we could get a late breakfast?" Only Vana could think about eating at a time like this.

"Oh, let's go to The Cove," said Audrey. "I hear it's delicious."

Vana, Lucy and I looked at each other and then laughed. "We love that place. In fact, it's the only place we've eaten at since we arrived."

"Great. And we'll take my car. I've seen yours," said Travis.

Vana bumped my shoulder with hers as we walked to the door. "It's about time," she whispered in my ear and flicked her eyes toward Travis.

The parking lot was so full when we arrived that Travis had to drive around twice until someone left. Fortunately, Tiffany was working this morning and seated us right away in front of one of the large picture windows and then left with our drink order.

"That girl looks so familiar to me," mused Audrey. "I wonder where I could have met her."

"I don't think so," said Vana as she perused the menu. "She said she's just in town visiting family."

The sound of conversation around us filtered through the air and made us hesitant to discuss our plans but we attempted it with quiet voices.

"Perhaps we should see if she had any rentals or a safety deposit box," suggested Lucy.

"I already checked for rental units," said Audrey. "And I've looked through her bank statements and there hasn't been any payments for that sort of thing. She did have a post office box but there's nothing there. She gave me power of attorney over her affairs when she got really ill. I guess I was the only one she could trust." She used her napkin to dab at her eyes.

"I don't think we should all go to the boat," I said. "It's too many people. Audrey, have you checked the post office box lately? Sometimes people mail things to themselves. Maybe she mailed the diary to herself to keep it safe."

Audrey shook her head no. "It's been awhile, what with the break-in at the house, I haven't thought about it. I don't know that I can access it on the weekend though."

"Vana, why don't you take Audrey to the post office, just in case it is open. Travis and I can go to the boat and Lucy can check title and see if Velma had any other properties or businesses. Is that okay with everyone?" I looked around at each of their faces for confirmation and received affirmative nods in response. We only had a few hours to find out as much information as we could. What if Shelby didn't show up at the airport? Hopefully, we would find her at the boat and the subterfuge wouldn't be necessary but it was nice to know we had backup just in case.

It might seem callous of us to be eating and working, but we all understand that in real estate you have to keep pushing forward or you flounder and get sucked up in the maelstrom that is life. Plus having something to do makes the time go faster. Sitting around worrying wouldn't help anyone.

"Lucy, look for properties by Carter or Goldie also. Her last name is Bergren. Hopefully, Carter Atley was stupid enough to use his real name."

A loud crash across the room, made us all spin our heads in that direction.

"That poor girl needs better spatial awareness," said Lucy sadly. Tiffany had managed to spill a whole tray of drinks; fortunately, not on the customers. "Waitressing doesn't look like a promising future for her."

I grimaced. "I believe those were our drinks. Oh, well." Of course now I was really thirsty. Psychology at its best, you want what you can't have.

Travis's phone buzzed and a smile lit his face as he looked at it. "Everything is in place. Hopefully, none of it will be necessary." His comment brought us a brief respite of hope. Tiffany arrived at our table shortly after with our drinks and then we spent the next half hour eating breakfast in silence each of us wound up in our own anxiety.

Audrey rose first, grabbing her coat and purse from the back of the chair. "Well then, I am getting the bill. No. No. No arguments. I got you into this mess, it's the least I can do." She cornered Tiffany across the room for the bill.

She rejoined us in the car. "I gave that poor girl an extra big tip. Hopefully, she doesn't have to pay for those broken glasses. Now let's get on with the adventure."

Travis dropped Lucy, Vana and Audrey at the house and then we proceeded on to the pier. The sun hadn't yet made an appearance today and the gloomy weather matched my mood. "How did I not know he was a bad fish?" I complained. "I'm usually such a good judge of character."

"That's what everyone thinks," replied Travis. "Bad guys don't always give off vibes. If they did, there wouldn't be so many murders or assaults." I had to admit he had something there. I would never have pegged Carol Whiteside as a murderer even after she had been proven to be one. She had just seemed like a sweet little old lady. I guess that just proved Travis's point.

"I guess they are just really good actors," I said grimacing at the thought. It made life so much more difficult and made me want to start questioning everyone's motives. How do people trust anyone with characters like that in the world?

"So what's our plan?" said Travis, changing the subject.

"Um."

"You don't have a plan do you?"

I pursed my lips. "Actually...no. This is my third trip to the boat and I haven't actually gotten to do any searching. Maybe that nice Captain Ahab will be there and can help us."

Travis's eyebrows rose to the roof at this comment. "Captain Ahab wasn't really a nice guy. Who is Captain Ahab?"

Laughing I said, "He's not really. He just dresses how I imagine Ahab would have looked. His name is really Patrick Flannagan and he is a nice guy." Was he really a nice guy? Did I need to reevaluate that in light of my new perspective on criminals? Was he a psycho in nice guy clothing?

"You're frowning."

I blew out the breath I didn't realize I was holding.

"You don't need to overthink it. The guy could actually be a nice person."

"How did you know what I was thinking?" I asked in shock.

This time Travis laughed. "I can read you like a book Holly. That's why I stayed away so long because I could see you weren't sure but when Audrey let me know the situation here, I had to come." He let out a breath and his face turned serious. "You bring light into my life Holly. You're the first person to do so since my wife passed.

I could think of nothing to say to that so I changed the subject and then kicked myself mentally for doing so. "If you thought you were being poisoned and you didn't want them to win, where would you hide your will?" I asked instead.

Travis wisely did the same. "Did you check inside all of her purses and coat pockets?"

"Wow, that's pretty insightful of you and yes we did. How did you think of that?"

"My wife used to hide extra cash in her pockets just in case she might need it."

"Well, I'm pretty sure it's not in the house. We were very thorough. The house is built on a hill so anything under it would have gotten washed out in the rain. Patrick said he searched the boat and found nothing." I raised my hands in a shrug.

The ring of my phone interrupted us. It was my granddaughter Chloe. "Nana, did you catch me a fish?"

"I sure did honey. As soon as I get home, I'll transfer it to you."

"Okay. Catch me some more please Nana."

"Of course, honey. I'm busy right now but I won't forget.

"That's the boat," I said pointing it out to him. It appeared to be empty.

"You keep a look out, I'm going to take a look around." He walked to the boat and slipped over the side. After he vanished, I walked to the end of the dock and gazed out at the water. The wind blew my hair around my face as I took a deep breath of the salty air and contemplated the events of the past two days. What was I doing? None of this had any relevance to me, not the body in the house or the missing heir, certainly not the possible poisoning. Did we leave tonight after finding Shelby? Should we extend our stay? None of us had a personal stake in any of this. But then, there was the sleuthing that I was beginning to enjoy plus the whole thing about helping people.

Maybe Audrey would be better off hiring a private detective but would she? She was just a friend. Velma's death had been ruled natural causes due to cancer so there would be no police investigation. Heck, they didn't even seem like they were really concerned about the dead body on the beach. If we didn't help, then who would find that poor missing child? My heart broke at the thought that Velma never got to meet her kid and now the kid may never find out what happened to her. I don't know why I kept thinking kid, they had to be grown by now. There had to be some way to find them, maybe a DNA match or something.

That got me thinking. Maybe Audrey could send away for a DNA kit and use Velma's hair from a brush. Maybe Velma had already done one. The first DNA test kits came out in 2000. I puffed my lips out in frustration. I would have done one if it was me. Maybe she had and the results were with the diary we couldn't find.

I would have to ask Audrey about it although I would think she would have said something. The pier was pretty desolate for a Sunday morning. Not even ole Bob was around. Travis slipped back over the boat railing and joined me on the dock, shaking his head.

"It was worth a shot," I said. "I guess we go back to the beach house and pack our stuff." Travis put his arm around my shoulders as we walked back to the car. The warmth of it felt comfortable. We were both silent on the ride back.

Lucy, Vana and Audrey looked up as we walked in. "Did you guys find out anything?" I asked.

"There was nothing in the post office box," said Audrey sadly.

I shrugged, "It was worth a try."

"Anybody want a drink?" asked Travis as he headed for the kitchen. After several affirmative responses he decided to make a pot of coffee.

"Do you think Goldie was trying to hide Charlie's body to delay the time of his death?" asked Lucy.

"There would be no point in that," called out Travis from the kitchen. "Unless Velma had a time clause in her will and Goldie would only know that if she had seen it." He poked his head back out. "When did Velma die?"

"Thursday morning," answered Audrey.

"And you ladies found the body on Friday?" We nodded in confirmation. He stepped all the way into the room. "What if Charlie died before Velma?"

"He wouldn't inherit," we all shouted at once. Travis pulled out his phone and made a call. Hanging up he said, "Coroner can't pinpoint the time of death beyond, early Thursday. Depending on when Velma passed, it could be contested as to who died first."

"So this puts Goldie clearly in the crosshairs. She hid Charlie's body so she could inherit Velma's money because he died too soon." It was only a theory, but it seemed a logical one. "Audrey, do you know if Velma ever did a DNA test through the mail?"

Audrey took a deep breath and blew it out slowly while she thought. "She was very secretive at the end." She shook her head. "It's possible. Nothing has come back through the post office box. Maybe there's something at her work? I just don't know."

Travis had disappeared back into the kitchen and came out bearing a tray of steaming cups of coffee. "I guess this means you definitely have to extend your stay. Once we get Shelby back of course."

"Raise your hand if you all agree," I said. All hands immediately shot up. "Great, I'll let my daughter know we're staying longer."

Audrey's eyes filled with tears. "Thank you so much. I feel I owe it to her to find her child."

"Let's go get Shelby back and then we'll find the kid," said Travis gently.

SUBTERFUGE

Lucy, Vana and I all lined up at the airport check-in, pulling our rolling cases behind us. My eyes scanned the airport until I felt a smack on my shoulder and Vana said, "Stop looking around, you almost knocked over that old man."

I looked up to see an elderly Chinese man glaring at me. I flashed him a quick smile in apology. He muttered something that sounded suspiciously like 'crazy Americans' and walked away.

As instructed we left a ticket for Shelby at the check-in stand. Once through the boarding gate, a woman pulled us aside and led us to a small room where we nervously waited for news.

If anything happened to Shelby, I would be devastated. The two of us had grown up together. She was my sister by another mother. What would I tell her daughter if something bad happened?

With nothing to do but wait, I ran different scenarios through my brain. "Can't you put out arrest warrants for Carter and Goldie?" I finally asked.

"We have no evidence to charge them with," interjected Travis. Always the voice of reason.

"He moved the body," Vana pointed out.

We have no proof of that," he said calmly.

It had to be him," insisted Lucy. "No one else was strong enough."

"What about Goldie and her son?" Asked Vana.

"No," I shook my head. "She was there too soon. Someone else had to drive the body away."

"It still could be them and the son drove the body away," suggested Travis.

"And carried it to the beach? I don't think so," I said.

Lucy was pacing back and forth across the floor. "I can't believe this is happening. How did this happen?"

"I'll tell you how it happened. You encouraged Holly to investigate. You were all excited about it and this is what happens," said Vana.

Lucy spun around to face her. "You can't possibly blame this on me. I didn't see you trying to stop her."

Vana rolled her eyes. "Holly is a force of nature. Nothing stops her."

"I'm sitting right here," I said. "Wait, what? I'm a what?" I frowned in Vana's direction. "You all encouraged me to do this. Shelby too. This is on all of us."

"I'm just saying that I've learned not to interfere when you get your mind set on something. That's all. If you would just use that power for yourself it might be better."

"Oh, so you're saying I just get myself into trouble all the time," I retorted.

Lucy was staring at the two of us, her hands on her hips. "What about getting covered in mud and almost getting killed by a psycho?"

"Mike was just angry." I pursed my lips as I remembered him coming after me with a crowbar. Okay, yeah, and a little psycho."

"Don't forget that woman who tried to murder you and Travis and Joanna," added Vana.

I looked at the two of them looking back at me with accusing eyes. "I was helping people. It's what I do. And you two wanted to help Audrey. We all did. You encouraged me to do this. Even Shelby did."

"Did what? What did I do?" Shelby was standing in the open door along with Scott and Travis. We ran to her at once and smothered her in a hug.

"I'm so sorry Shelby, that I got you into this. Are you okay," I cried.

"You didn't get me into anything Holly. I walked into this and I'm fine."

"What happened to you. Was it Carter? Did he kidnap you?" asked Lucy.

"Kidnapping. What kidnapping?" she asked, puzzled.

Vana intervened at this moment. "Ladies, give her some breathing room. Everyone sit down so she can give us all the details."

We all sat down. Strangely, Shelby didn't seem as shook up as I thought she should be. She began her story. "Carter texted me and we went for a drive up the coast. We had car trouble and had to wait for a tow truck. He finally got a text from Audrey that you were all leaving and would meet me at the airport. What's going on?"

"You went on a date with him after that conversation at the movies?" I exclaimed in frustration. I'll admit I was angry at the news and part of me felt let down and disappointed. "Wait, who has your phone?"

Shelby shook her head negatively. "I don't know. I can't find it anywhere."

My mind was going a mile a minute. "Where's Carter?"

"He just dropped me off. Why? What is going on? Why are you acting all crazy and why is Scott here?"

We all sat and stared at each other, if Audrey texted Carter, she had to know something, right? Travis finally broke the silence saying what we were all thinking. "I don't know what's going on but Audrey would never do anything like this."

"Like what?" I asked.

"Whatever this is," he said, waving his hand around. I know she's not involved. She's a good person. Someone must have just gotten a hold of her phone."

I turned to Shelby and asked again, "Where's Carter now?"

She shrugged in frustration. "I don't know. He dropped me off and left. Why are you all in this room? Are we leaving?"

I took a deep breath and filled her in on what had happened then asked, "Do you think Carter deliberately kept you out to get us to leave?"

Shelby looked shocked and then frowned. "Why would he do that? He's a nice guy."

Travis and Scott both looked at each other and then at her. "Shelby," began Travis. "There's no Carter Atley working for the police department. We think he's a con man, possibly working with Goldie. They think there's millions of dollars up for grabs. That's a lot of motive."

"They think?" she asked, picking up on the words.

Vana reached over and took her hands. "We don't think they know about the trust."

Shelby was shaking her head sadly. "I can't believe that. Carter seems like such a great guy. He explained how he was a little shaken up about the whole situation and me being in danger and he wasn't able to help." She looked up at Travis and Scott. "He's not with the police?"

"No, not that we could find. That doesn't appear to be his real name either."

"This is crazy," she said. "We've got to find that poor kid before they do. Do they know she was looking for her child? Do we know who the father is? Who gets the money if the kid dies?" She shot out the questions rapid fire, giving us no time to respond.

Those were all good questions. Who did get the money? Without the will there was no way to find out. Travis was right, millions of dollars makes a good motive and Goldie seemed capable of anything. I had closed my eyes while I was thinking and now I looked back up at them.

"Has Goldie actually done anything? I mean, if Velma really did die from cancer and Charlie from a heart attack, then she's only guilty of moving a dead man. Is that even a crime?"

Scott grimaced, "Actually, it is. If the coroner can't prove that Charlie died before Velma, there's a very good chance that Goldie could get the courts to award her the money, if there are no other blood relatives."

"Audrey's the trustee, I know she'll fight to prevent Goldie from getting it but if there's no actual proof that this child exists, well," he shrugged helplessly.

"Isn't there a birth certificate?" I asked, looking at Travis. Something about his demeanor was setting me off. "What are you not telling us?"

Instead of answering, he deflected. "I think we need to go find Audrey. Maybe she can answer these questions."

Vana gave Shelby another quick hug as we exited the room. "Oh, and Shelbs, we're staying a few more days."

"Great," she answered but it wasn't enthusiastically which reinforced my decision to find out what was going on with her.

TRUTH

Audrey squirmed in her seat. She had met us at the beach house. "I know you said you and Velma were good friends but I think it was more than that. Why are you so invested in finding this child?" I didn't mean to sound like an interrogator, but I'm afraid it came out that way, sounding harsher than I meant it to.

"I did a dreadful thing," she said, wringing her hands. "I, I encouraged Velma to give up her child. It was for the best," she muttered in defense. "At the time, I thought it was the right thing to do for her. But, now I realize, maybe it wasn't.

"She said she never regretted it and that she was glad her child had the chance for a better life. It was because of the cancer diagnosis that she really wanted to find the child, just in case it was genetic. It wasn't till the end that she questioned her diagnosis. I don't know what made her suspicious. I asked but she wouldn't say. She didn't want me to get hurt. But she made me promise to find the child."

Audrey stopped speaking and sat in the chair with her eyes scrunched up tight, her hands in a fist in her lap. "That's what I don't understand," she burst out. "If she wanted me to find the baby, why didn't she leave me any information? I've looked and looked and I just can't find anything."

Lucy smiled kindly at her. "I'm great with searches. It's my job, it's what I do all day long. Let's start at the beginning. Do you know when the baby was born?"

Audrey sniffled and looked up at her with hope. "Um, it would have been 25 years ago, in March I believe. I don't know who the father was. Does that help?"

"Daughter," I interrupted.

"What?"

"Nick referred to the kid as 'she'," I said.

"Well that eliminates half the population," said Lucy.

"First thing tomorrow, we'll start searching through records. Can you go to her place of work and see if there's anything there? Maybe she left a clue in her desk."

"Shelby and I will go with you," volunteered Vana.

"Great," I said. "I'll go with Scott and Travis and we can look for Carter and Goldie. One of them was behind all this."

"I don't know," interrupted Audrey as she looked in my direction. "Are you sure you want to leave her alone with Travis?"

It took us all a moment to get the joke and then we all burst out laughing. "I'm glad you haven't lost your sense of humor," remarked Shelby.

"There's nothing more we can do tonight so why don't we have a nice dinner and just enjoy the beach. That is after all what we came here for." I looked around the room at each one of my friends. "And no one goes anywhere alone."

"Agreed," they all said.

"Let's get pizza," I suggested. "What kind do you want?"

"Anchovie and mushroom," piped in Shelby.

We all looked at her like she had gone mad. "Are you pregnant?" questioned Vana.

"What? You've never had fungus and fish?" she asked. "It's delicious, the salty with the mushrooms."

"Are you serious right now?" asked Lucy. "I'm thinking veggie and a pepperoni and sausage."

"Fine, I'll have what you want," she said, disgruntled. "But you don't know what you're missing."

"I'll speak for all of us, when I say we're fine missing it," I added.

We ordered out for pizza and beer and spent the next few hours just enjoying ourselves. The late afternoon melted into evening and we enjoyed a beautiful sunset with old friends and new.

Early the next morning, I stepped onto the balcony, coffee in hand, then froze. A few drops of coffee sloshed over the side of my cup as I slowly backed up and fumbled behind me for the door knob. As soon as I was through, I slammed the door and locked it.

"Shelby!" I screamed. "Shelby! You get in here now!"

Shelby along with everyone else ran into the living room. She was still trying to wrap her floral satin robe around her silk pajamas when she asked nervously, "what is it? What's wrong?"

I raised a shaking hand to point out the kitchen window. "Did you do this?" Outside on the railing seagulls were lined up wing to wing with more landing every second, jostling for position. Bird poop was scattered across the chairs and balcony. Her mouth dropped open and then she began protesting. "It was just a few chips, honestly. Oh my, Lucy, I'm so sorry I'll clean up everything."

"Just a few chips?" I said accusingly, frowning at her, as I recalled all the times she was the last to come in.

"Okay, maybe some muffins and other things," she mumbled.

The rest of us had a quick breakfast of juice, muffins and fruit while Shelby shooed the birds away and cleaned up the balcony.

"We're going to need to go to the store if we plan on staying longer," advised Lucy.

Travis had spent the night on the couch and Scott had taken Audrey home. They were going to join us this morning so we could make plans.

TRUST

"Let's go back to the beginning," I said, from my seat on the living room couch. "You said, there's a trust. Doesn't that have to be done by a lawyer?"

"Yes, it does," said Audrey, sitting up from the couch. "His name is Calvin Tremont."

I smiled. "Then we should pay him a visit."

With plans changed, it was decided that Audrey, Shelby, Vana and I would visit the lawyer, then go by Velma's office. Scott and Travis would drop off Lucy to do a records search while they visited the local precinct and conducted a search for Goldie and Carter. It didn't really take four of us but I felt that Audrey needed the support and we weren't letting Shelby out of our sight.

The lawyer's office was located in a posh building in the center of town. As we pulled into the parking garage, there was a beige Mercedes parked near the elevators. "Do you see that?" I hissed to the other girls.

"See what?" asked Vana.

"Not you, you have to focus on driving," I replied.

"Then don't have an open ended question," she snapped.

"Shelby, Audrey," I spoke very dramatically and slowly emphasizing their names. "Did you see that beige Mercedes?" I pointed back down the aisle. From the corner of my eye I caught Vana looking in the rear view mirror. "What's the point of specifying names, Vana, if you're just going to look anyway?"

"Hmph," was all she said, but she snapped her eyes forward again. Then, just to be facetious, she drove around the garage and back by the Mercedes. "It does look like the same car." I glared at her.

Audrey spoke up quickly to distract us. "We're by the beach. I'm sure there's a lot of Mercedes around here.

"I don't know," mused Shelby. "It does look similar."

"Can we please park," I whined. "I need to stretch my legs." This back seat wasn't doing me any favors, especially since Shelby had moved her seat back to accommodate her long legs. We all clambered out of the car and made our way to the elevator in the corner.

The lawyer's office was as you might expect, filled with leather furniture and a beautiful view of the skyline from the sixth floor. Calvin Tremont has in his sixties with gray thinning hair and a muffin top held up by suspenders over his classic white button up shirt and black slacks. He eased himself into the leather chair behind the desk as we filed into the room and took seats.

I explained to him about Velma and the missing diary and will and then waited for him to speak.

He let out a deep sigh. "It's gone."

On a hunch I showed him the picture on the phone.

"That's my girlfriend," he said. Then it hit me.

"You were at the movies with Goldie and her son."

"Yes, my crazy ex-wife tried to shoot me."

I pursed my lips in a frown. "No. The boy said she was trying to kill your girlfriend."

"Goldie," we all said at the same time.

"She had proof that my wife was cheating on me," said Calvin.

"With this guy?" I showed him the picture of Carter and his eyes opened wide.

"Yeah, that's the guy."

We looked at each other, "she stole it."

Calvin looked at each of us dubiously. "Are you saying Goldie dated me so she could steal the will?"

I licked my lips nervously. "What kind of proof did she have about your wife?" I asked.

He narrowed his eyes at us. "She had pictures of that guy and my wife in compromising positions. Why? What are you thinking?"

"It's possible she faked them." I felt sorry for the guy. He was dealing with a master manipulator and didn't realize it. "How long have you been dating?"

"About a month," he said with a sigh. "What could I do? She was my wife. She swore the pictures weren't real but I could see that they were. If this is true, though, I guess I'll have to forgive her. Wait, you said the boy?"

I stared at him for a moment. He thought his ex-wife tried to kill him. "She didn't shoot at you," I said slowly. "It was your son. Your wife manipulated him into it. Why would you forgive her?"

Shock, then anger and sadness passed over his face, before his shoulders slumped and he frowned at the desk. I have never seen a man so broken in that moment as he sat staring at the top of the desk and I hope to never see it again. I gave him a moment, then said, "I am so sorry, Mr. Tremont. I do have to ask though, when did you find out that the will was missing?"

Calvin finally looked up, "When Velma passed away, I was notified. I came into the office and checked the file but it wasn't there. I thought maybe it was just misplaced so I had my secretary look for it. She went through every file but it's gone. I'm sorry."

"So what happens if the will can't be found," inquired Audrey.

Calvin gave a small shrug to his shoulders, "I seem to recall the house is in the trust?" At Audrey's affirmative nod, he continued on. "Then whatever is outside the trust will have to go through probate. A search for heirs will be conducted. It could take a while."

"Just one more question. Do you remember if Velma named a beneficiary in the will?"

"I gave her a copy of the will and, here's the funny thing, she named the beneficiary and put the name in a sealed envelope and then signed over the flap and I notarized the envelope. I don't know who it was, but she did leave everything in a trust for whoever she named in the envelope, with Audrey here as Trustee."

Great, we were back to square one of knowing nothing. We all looked at each other grimly. "Well, thank you Mr. Tremont," I said, standing to shake his hand. "I'm terribly sorry about what happened with your son."

We left him sitting behind the desk and showed ourselves out, nodding to the secretary as we passed her desk in the outer office.

"Do you think Goldie knows about the kid and that's why she's moving on? Hedging her bets? Or was it just to steal the will?" We had barely entered the elevator before Vana started asking questions.

"I wish I knew," I sighed, pushing the button for the ground floor where our car was. We headed straight over to Velma's office but like everything else, it yielded no clues. It was just one dead end after another. We headed back to the beach house hoping that Lucy or Travis and Scott had better luck.

THOUGHTS

I woke up in the early morning hours, unable to sleep. Wrapping a blanket around me, I made my way through the quiet house and out to the balcony. Thankfully, there were no birds around. Travis was snoring softly on the couch. He hadn't wanted to leave after the events of the evening. The reflection of the full moon glittered in silver on the ocean. It was so peaceful and quiet, it was hard to believe anything bad could happen here.

A quiet footstep alerted me that someone was up, a moment before Travis appeared. "Couldn't sleep huh?" He came over and wrapped me in a warm hug before stepping away. "Sorry, we didn't have better news."

Neither Travis, Scott nor Lucy had found anything useful. At least the sunrise was beautiful. Travis went back inside to make coffee leaving me alone with my thoughts. Two cups of coffee later and the rest of the household was awake. The smell of bacon and eggs wafted through the air to me and I went inside to find Vana and Lucy cooking breakfast.

"We have to go back to Mr. Zimmerman's," I said suddenly.

"Why?" Whined Vana. "He was such a warm, caring man. Plus he's been retired for two years."

"Does he still get money from the practice?"

Vana gave me a sheepish look. "I don't know."

"Money is a big incentive. We only know what people told us. We need confirmation of some facts." I snagged a piece of bacon off the plate and went to my room to get dressed.

Entering the living room again, this time fully dressed, Vana took one look at me and said, "You're wearing that? I thought we were real estate agents."

"We are but I'm not taking any chances," I said, defending my clothing choice of jeans and a T-shirt. I soon regretted my words as the girls took it upon themselves to retell the story in minute detail for Travis over breakfast. They were laughing so hard, I was afraid they were going to have a stroke.

REVELATIONS

Something was bothering me and I couldn't pinpoint what it was. The more I thought about it the more it slipped away like an elusive fish. If I couldn't help myself, at least I could help Chloe. "I'm going outside to fish," I said as I grabbed my phone and walked outside. If I didn't think, maybe it would come to me.

"Holly fishes?" asked Travis.

"It's a game," replied Lucy. Their voices faded away as I shut the door behind me.

I opened the game and spun the ball but this fish was tough and I soon ran out of balls. That's when I remembered the gift from Carter. I opened it and then paused before taking a screenshot of it. Chloe's fish would have to wait.

With a smile on my face, I walked back inside. The girls had all left the room and it was just Travis sitting on the couch. I showed him the photo on my phone and his smile joined mine.

"I can work with that," he said. Just then all of our phones pinged as Vana texted us to meet her in the driveway. I hadn't even known she'd left.

As we exited the front door, Vana pulled up in an electric jeep. "I checked back and they had this," she said.

Amazingly, Shelby looked sad. "What?" she exclaimed when she realized I was staring at her. "I kinda liked that car. I think I might buy one when we get back."

"In the snow?" I questioned.

"Hey, It's not snowing all the time. It'll be a great little car the other three seasons. Imagine it, driving through the forest, the top down, enjoying an unhindered view."

"So you're getting a convertible now," stated Lucy. "Hmm, that does sound nice."

"Sure," retorted Vana, "Pine cones falling on your head."

"You don't have to like it, it's my car. Admit it, you really love the idea, you're just being annoying for no good reason," said Shelby.

Vana laughed. "Yes. I'm sorry, it does sound like fun." She added, "Travis said you had a lead."

Comprehension set in and I nodded my head, "Yes, we do." I had Shelby text Carter to meet us at the restaurant bar at noon. He was either overly confident or an idiot, because he agreed to do so.

ZIMMERMAN

Vana drove us to Harold Zimmerman's in the much more comfortable and spacious car in which I once again got to sit in the front passenger seat. I knocked on his door and then stepped to the side. I wasn't taking any chances with the dog today. Not with Travis and Audrey watching. They had parked just past the house on the opposite side of the road and Lucy and Shelby were waiting in the car again just up the road from the house on the same side of the street.

"Oh, it's you again," he said cheerfully. "Come in, come in. Did you find the answers you were looking for?"

I hesitated to enter under false pretenses, so I told him the truth. "Mr. Zimmerman, Vana and I aren't really looking for a home for buyers," I said. "Really, we're looking into the death of Velma DiAngelo. Her friend Audrey told us you diagnosed her."

"I know," he said. "We're a close knit community here and you didn't visit anyone else. Please do come in. I put Siegfried in the backyard when I saw you pull up."

I waved to the girls in the car and we went inside to his comfortable living room. I finally had a chance to actually see it this time. There were flowered couches and chintz curtains. It looked very comfortable and feminine and totally out of date. Harold saw me admiring the furniture.

"My wife decorated and it makes me feel close to her," he said with a sad smile.

"It's hard when a loved one passes," I said in sympathy. Harold sat in a chair by the window and I sat on the couch but Vana kept standing. "Would you mind if I used your restroom? I had too much coffee this morning."

"Of course, it's just down the hall. Just please don't leave dirt under my rug." He gave me a knowing look and I felt my face burning.

Vana gave him a puzzled look and walked down the hall. "I'm really sorry about that," I began when he cut me off.

"No worries. It was my dog's fault to begin with. Sometimes, I like to joke to make my patients comfortable. Now what did you need to know about Velma?"

I explained to him about Audrey and her concerns and why we had suspicions. Vana came back and sat down beside me.

"I can assure you, she did have cancer, but I will look into the protocols used. If anything unethical was done, I will bring charges against her. This is the most reprehensible thing a doctor can do to a patient." He sat with his shoulders slumped. I could imagine after what his wife went through how this accusation would hit him hard.

"I saw the picture on the wall, were you and Velma close friends?" I asked. He looked toward the wall that held the picture as he remembered the one in question.

"Velma was also the name of my wife. I sold the boat to Charlie and Velma after she passed and they would include me on trips. We both loved fishing, me and Charlie. You know they used to be high school sweethearts and then they drifted apart and years later found each other again. My wife just loved that story. So romantic she said." His voice trailed off as he remembered his wife and a sad look crossed over his face. "Anyway, he promised to never change the name. I came back to the office to diagnose her. It was just a terrible day but I wanted the news to come from me."

"That must have been very hard," said Vana. "Having to tell your friend she hasn't long to live. What was your prognosis, if you don't mind me asking?"

"I suppose it's all right now. She had less than a year. The cancer had already spread to her lymph nodes and organs. I believe she stopped treatment at the end."

"Why would she do that?" I asked, shocked. I would have fought til the very end for my daughter and granddaughter.

Harold stared at the floor with a sad smile on his face. "Some patients do. They are tired of the pain and make peace with the end. Velma was a strong woman, like my wife. It's hard to make that choice."

I took a breath before speaking. "I'm so sorry you had to go through that again. I understand she got divorced after the diagnosis?"

"It was terrible, the divorce. I believe a husband should support his wife, no matter what." Harold shook his head sadly. "I think Velma thought it would make it easier for Charlie to move on after she passed. She encouraged the relationship with Goldie who was only too happy to snatch him up. I think his heart was still broken when she passed."

Wow, I had it all wrong. Charlie wasn't the philanderer I thought he was. That brought into question Audrey. Should we be trusting what she told us? If this information was wrong, what other incorrect information had she passed on to us? I had seen her ID, she was definitely the right Audrey, but what did we really know about her?

"You look like you've got a lot on your mind." Vana's observation brought me out of my reverie. Looking around, I realized we were nearly to the beach house. She had already explained to the rest of the group over the speaker phone what Harold had said. I had tuned out the conversation and was wrapped up in my own thoughts.

"Why would Audrey ask four total strangers to help her out? Do we look that trustworthy?" And why did she hesitate when we asked her about searching the house," I asked after Vana disconnected the call.

"Maybe she did it to divert suspicion," said Shelby from the front passenger seat. She had snagged it when we left the car. "She was really open with her answers."

"She is Travis's cousin," said Lucy seated next to me, "and he seems to trust her." And that was the problem. I trusted Travis so it seemed like I should trust his opinion but doubts nagged at me. Why did she hesitate when we asked her about searching for the diary? She was already the trustee, she already had control of all the money. Did she know what was in the will? Did she lose the money if the child was found? How well did Travis really know his cousin?

CARTER

It was decided that Travis and I would confront Carter. Scott had another investigation to attend to. Audrey had clients to meet and the rest of us didn't want to leave Shelby alone, so Lucy and Vana stayed at the house with her.

Travis drove the short distance to the restaurant but I lacked the courage to confront him about Audrey. Did she call him in to keep an eye on me? He hadn't really shown that much of an interest in me before but now all of a sudden he was in love? If I had to admit it, a large part of me was hoping that none of this was true.

"We're here," he said as he shut off the car. "Are you ready?" I looked into his face and I began to doubt my doubts. He had always been honest with me.

"Yeah, let's go." I gave him a nervous smile and we both walked to the restaurant entrance. We spotted Carter in a booth by one of the picture windows overlooking the ocean. The restaurant was nearly full with customers both inside and out on the patio.

Carter turned to look at the door as we walked in and his face fell. Travis and I sat on either side of him pinning him in the booth.

"Hello Carter," I said. "Sorry, Shelby isn't coming."

"What do you want?" he asked, turning to face his half full mug of beer.

"Holly has an interesting story, she'd like to tell you," said Travis. "I suggest you listen."

Carter took a long draught of his beer, then wiped his mouth with his fist. "Go for it, I got time."

"It starts with an open house and a guy with a heart attack and then ends with you pulling a weekend at Bernie's and moving the dead guy to the beach. You do know that's a crime right?" I asked.

"You can't prove I was there," he snarled. I smiled at him as I pulled up a photo on my phone and set it on the table sliding it over to him.

"With that photo, I have cause to have you arrested," said Travis, nodding at my phone.

Shock crossed Carter's face and then resignation. "What do you want to know?"

"Where's the diary?" I asked.

Carter waved his hands in front of his face. "Okay, okay. Let's make a deal here."

I crossed my arms over my chest and leaned against my seat back. Of course he wants to make a deal now when he's caught. Travis tipped his chin at Carter. "What have you got?"

"It was all Goldie's doing. Charlie had a heart attack Thursday morning and then the hospital called the house to let Charlie know Velma had died. Goldie took the call. She thought she could make it look like he had died after Velma so she could still inherit the money."

"Too bad there isn't any money," I said.

"What do you mean?" I now had Carter's full attention as he narrowed his eyes at me.

"Velma put her money in a trust and it wasn't going to Charlie."

"Are you kidding me right now?" he said, laughing.

"Where's Goldie?"

"Look man, I don't know. I'd tell you if I did. Like I said, I don't care for that chick."

"And Velma's diary?"

Carter shook his head. "I don't know anything about that."

"Don't go anywhere," said Travis as he got up from the table and motioned me to join him. He pulled across the restaurant floor to the bar.

"What are you doing? He's right there."

"We have to let him go."

"What?" I exclaimed.

"We have no evidence that he did anything other than move a dead body. The person we really want is Goldie. I think we need to focus on that."

I took a deep breath and let it out slowly to center myself. Then returned to Carter. "What can you give us on Goldie?" I asked in my best negotiating voice.

Carter narrowed his eyes at me as he scrutinized my face, before he came to a decision. "Okay, I'll be straight with you. Goldie was paying me to help her. You gotta believe I was only in it for the money. If any woman is a black widow, then that chick is, if you know what I mean." He took another long drink from his beer, draining the mug.

"Frankly, she scares me. She's hot and all but she's not worth doing time for. Only thing is, I never saw her do anything illegal. I don't think she has the diary either. She's been really mad over the whole Charlie dying thing. She made me search the house and the boat. There's nothing there. IF there is a diary I haven't seen it. Maybe ask the kid. Him and Velma were apparently friends."

I slapped my hand down on the table in frustration. "Great. Thanks. I'll do that."

I kept my tongue until we made it outside and then I vented my frustration. "That's just great! We have exactly nothing."

"We may have something," said Travis quietly. The tone of his voice made me look at him suspiciously.

"What did you get from that conversation?"

"He said he thinks she's a black widow."

"So?"

"So, maybe this isn't her first time."

I closed my eyes for a moment to calm myself. I opened them and said, "You think she poisoned Velma and killed Charlie." It wasn't a question.

"I think it's highly possible that she's more skilled than we thought and she needs to be behind bars." He looped his arm through mine and escorted me back to the Jeep. Once inside, he started the car but didn't move it.

"What are you thinking?" I asked.

"I'm thinking that maybe we can get Carter and plan a trap for Goldie."

"Um, isn't that a little like interfering with a police investigation?" I asked innocently.

Travis gave me a long hard look and I found it difficult to maintain a straight face. My lips gave me away when the edges ticked up in a smile. "Very funny. The truth is, they aren't even investigating anymore. It can't be interference if there's no investigation."

Travis shut off the vehicle and we went back inside to speak to Carter again.

"SO WHAT'S THE PLAN?" asked Vana after we filled them in on what happened.

"Carter is going to renegotiate his deal. Hopefully, it will make Goldie panic. Especially when he tells her there's no money coming."

"How sure are we that she doesn't already know that?" Asked Shelby, her hands on her hips. "Maybe we should just call it quits and go home?"

I looked at her in disbelief. "How can you say that? We just got proof that she's been dishonest."

"Did we though?" questioned Shelby.

"Shelby, sure he's hot, but you need to get your head out of the clouds. This guy is trouble. He's committing crimes," I scolded her.

"Ladies, we need to get back on track," said Travis calmly. "Shelby, I admit the guy is hot but Holly is right, he's going to jail. For how long depends on whether he can catch Goldie or not. So let's focus on that. That is how you help him."

Shelby glared at all of us and then sat down with her arms crossed over her chest. I still had the business card the realtor had given us from the second open house and we arranged a private showing for Goldie and Carter.

Carter called us on his phone and we listened in while he talked to her. Let's just say he took a few liberties with the truth.

"The agent really said he would lower the price for me? You know how much I really want this house."

"Only if we can get the deal closed by the end of the week."

There was some silence and then, "Tell the agent yes."

"Okay, but where are you going to get the money from? I thought you were broke. Wait, are you getting it from the lawyer?"

"Oh, honey, don't you worry about that. I've got money stashed away. Let's just say my previous husbands took good care of me before they died."

"That's great. Just one more thing."

"And what's that darling?"

There were some muffled sounds that I didn't want to guess what they were and then Carter said, "I think I'm going to need some more money. I didn't agree to moving a dead body. Did you have something to do with Charlie keeling over?"

We heard what definitely sounded like a slap and then, "How dare you ask me that! Do you know how much trouble that's caused me by him dying before Velma? His timing couldn't have been worse. Why couldn't he have been like my other husbands and die right on time?"

"What are you? Like a black widow or something?"

"Oh honey, don't you worry about that. As long as you don't marry me, you should be just fine. Now call that agent and wrap this up for me, darling. Don't worry about the money, I'll make sure you get what's coming to you."

"You'd better."

We were parked in a driveway a few houses down and watched as Carter left the house a few moments later and returned to his car. He took off down the road like he was being chased. Goldie exited five minutes later and got into the beige Mercedes, probably admiring her future home one last time. Too bad, her next house was going to come with bars.

"Did we get what we needed?" I asked Travis.

"We might have enough to get exhumation orders for her previous marriages. His words left me disappointed. After all this, we still had to just wait and watch her walk away.

"We didn't even get any information about the diary," I said disgruntled. Travis reached over and grabbed my hand.

"Sometimes, it happens this way. Trust the process."

I pulled my hand from his in frustration.

Travis dropped me at the beach house with some final words. "I'm going to go back to the local precinct and do some research. Maybe they'll listen to us now. You guys stay here, enjoy the beach until I get back."

I smiled and nodded but I had absolutely no intention of doing either of those things. Instead I went inside and convinced the girls to go on a stake out with me. The plan was to check Charlie's house first. If she really thought she was going to get the new house then she would definitely start packing up. She didn't strike me as a wait around kind of gal.

We all grabbed some snacks and drinks and Shelby brought along a bucket which she put on the floor between her feet.

"Okay, I give," said Vana finally. "What is the bucket for?"

"Well," began Shelby, "we don't know how long we're going to be sitting in the car for and we may need to go pee."

"Euww no!" said Lucy. "I am not using that bucket. Besides, you forgot toilet paper."

Shelby raised her eyebrows, "Did I?" She reached into her backpack and pulled out a roll.

"Oh, heck no," exclaimed Vana. "I will keep my legs crossed before I use that. And no one else is using it in this car either."

"Suit yourself," said Shelby calmly, causing me to question what she could have been doing before in order to know this.

A sudden thought crossed my mind. "Hey Lucy, can you look up where the lawyer lives?"

She pulled her phone out of her bag and began tapping on her phone. "What are you thinking?"

"Well, his wife is in jail so maybe she is staying there."

"Good thinking," said Vana.

"And if she is, we won't have to use Shelby's toilet," I added. I could feel Shelby rolling her eyes in the seat behind me.

"Got it. 21240 Livesey Court."

Vana punched in the address before I had a chance to react. "It's 20 minutes away. Keep an eye out for her car."

"Might I remind you Lucy, that you're the one that wanted to use a sink in the escape room," said Shelby.

"It's not a bucket," she replied.

"Can we just move on? Look for that car," I reprimanded them as if they were children.

As Vana drove, we all scanned the nearby roads for Goldie's beige Mercedes. Actually, I wasn't even sure it was hers but she continued to drive it.

Unfortunately, we didn't find it at the doctor's house or his office. "Looks like you might need my bucket after all," said Shelby nonchalantly.

Our plan went awry as we were stopped at a red light and Goldie pulled up next to our car in her SUV.

She glanced in our direction as she passed us and flipped out, taking off in her SUV. It never having dawned on us that she might switch cars.

"I think she saw us," said Vana, the understatement of the year, as she stomped on the gas pedal.

"Don't lose her," yelled Shelby just as Lucy yelled, "slow down." Needless to say, Vana did not slow down. Goldie careened around a Mercedes and her rear tires slid on the asphalt as she turned into the parking on the beach.

"Where does she think she's going," asked Lucy hanging onto the grip bar above the door as Vana made the turn just a hair more carefully, but still way too fast for our comfort. I was trying to keep an eye on Goldie, when I heard Vana say, "thank goodness we've got a Jeep."

"Wha..?" I began when she jerked the wheel to cut off Goldie's exit from the parking lot. Instead Goldie zipped along the pedestrian walkway onto the sand. It was low tide and a huge expanse of damp sand was before us. I was caught between the horror of watching or hiding my head in case we crashed.

"I don't think this is what Travis had in mind!" I finally yelled but Vana took no notice. She usually doesn't when she's driving. Goldie was weaving back and forth between the dry sand and the surf. Beachgoers were dashing to get out of her way. Where were the lifeguards when you needed them?

"She's gonna have to do something now. Look," said Lucy pointing to the rock berm ahead. A flash of red and blue lights caught my eye to the left and Goldie swerved towards the surf. Determined not to let her get away, Vana punched the gas pedal and the Jeep shot out into the surf cutting her off.

In horror, Shelby cried out, "didn't you say this was an electric vehicle?"

"Yeah, why?" asked Vana as the water crashed over the hood.

"Because electric batteries catch fire when they get wet," she screamed. We all glanced at each other with wide eyes before we each shoved our doors open and ran away from the car. All except Shelby who was now really angry. We watched in awe as she ran to Goldie's now floating car and yanked the door open, pulling Goldie out by her hair.

It's pretty hard to run away when someone's got your hair in their hands. The police had stopped their vehicle safely on the sand and now confronted Shelby and Goldie. Shivering in the cold and our wet clothes we walked over to the police to face our fates.

"I'm pretty sure she killed two people and possibly more," said Shelby. "You'd better lock her up."

It was nearly an hour later when Travis showed up where we were sitting on the sand above high tide with our hands cuffed behind our backs. I could tell he was angry by the stiffness in his shoulders and the clenched jaw.

"He doesn't look happy, does he," asked Shelby. "Do you think he can get them to take the cuffs off? My shoulders are starting to ache."

"Uh, oh, that can't be good," I said as the officers glanced in our direction and started laughing.

They finally came over with Travis and released us into his custody. "I'm letting you go as long as you leave the area by tomorrow," said an officer with dark hair. Worst of all they did the same to Goldie, except she lived here so she didn't have to leave the area.

Vana was on the phone with the car rental agency and I could tell it wasn't going well. I was cold and wet and miserable. Could this day get any worse?

"Holly, hi, good to see you again." I turned to see Larry from the worst date ever, still wearing a T-shirt and board shorts with his socks and sandals.

"Hi Larry,"

"Barry," he corrected me.

"Hi, I'm Barry," he said and extended his hand toward Travis who shook it. "Are you two on a date?" he asked, sounding a bit hurt as he said the words.

"Um, no, Barry. This is Travis, we have business together and we really need to get going. Nice to see you again." He tried to hug me but I dodged it. I could feel my face burning. I snagged Travis's arm and turned him as we walked away.

"Okay, bye," called Barry after us. "Call me if you want to do dinner again."

What were the chances of running into Barry after our date? And why right now? Sometimes the only luck I have is bad. I could feel Travis's eyes burning a hole in the side of my head but I refused to look up.

"Holly?"

"Yeah?"

"Did you go on a date?" His sudden stop forced me to stop as well or fall headlong on the ground as I was still holding onto his arm.

A queasiness entered my stomach as I looked up at him. Did he look a little hurt? He put a finger on my lips before I could speak and started walking again. "It doesn't matter. It's none of my business."

He abruptly stopped again and swung me around to face him. "It's just that you've only been out here for a few days. And you went on a date?" He looked dumbfounded. "I mean how did you even meet?"

I bit my lip and then the words all came out in a rush. "It was Lucy. I promised she could choose my next date and, and she, she, I don't even know how, found me a date here like we even have time to date, what with finding a dead body and everything. And it was awful, he was awful. I'm sorry," I blurted out and raised my eyes to see that Barry had followed us and heard every word.

"I'm sorry Barry, You weren't the worst date ever." I lied to make him feel better.

"I just need to get in here," he mumbled and pushed past me to open the door to the car we were standing in front of. Why did that make me feel worse?

I looked back to see Travis frowning at me. Can the ground just swallow me up right now? I tried to wave goodbye to Barry as he backed up but he averted his gaze and I just felt foolish.

"What were you thinking Holly? I thought you had more sense than this."

"I'm sorry about the date, I didn't know you were interested."

"Not the date," he said angrily. "Following Goldie. You know we don't have anything on her. Now she's going to run and that's on you. This is why amateurs shouldn't get involved in police work."

"Oh, right," I said, now angry myself. "What was with all that talk about helping me? At least now I know how you really feel. And what about your cousin?"

"What about her?" Confusion was written all over his face at this change in subject.

"How do you know she's not involved? She was looking for the diary and she's in charge of the trust. Maybe she doesn't really want to find the kid so she can keep the money herself."

I knew I should stop talking but I just couldn't. "What kind of a person asks four random strangers to help them?"

Travis squeezed his eyes closed, shaking his head, then he opened them and walked away. Fine, let him be mad. What kind of a guy walks away at the first sign of trouble? I need that kind of person in my life. That's what I thought, but I also desperately wanted to call after him. I wanted him to stop and come back; tell me everything was just a mistake, but he didn't. Instead, the girls came up and let me know an uber was on the way.

The car rental company had refused to give us another vehicle so we were relegated to using a ride share service. We went back to the beach house and showered and changed. I cried in the shower until the water ran cold and Vana pounded on the door and threatened to come in if I didn't come out soon. We packed our clothes and Lucy got us plane tickets for the next afternoon.

We had one last meal at the restaurant. The older waitress took our order. "Where's Tiffany?"

She was standing with her pen in her hand ready to take our order. "She's going back home tomorrow."

"Oh, Did she have a nice visit with her mom, Doris," I said, reading her name off of her tag pinned to her top.

"She said it wasn't the conversation she wanted to have. She seemed a little sad when she left. She's really had a tough time here."

"Oh? How so?" asked Vana.

"A girl in the parking lot got hit by a car and died just after she started working here. Poor Tiff watched the whole thing happen." Doris dropped her voice to a whisper. "And between you and me, she's not made out for waitressing." She gave us a knowing look. "And the whole thing with not being able to connect with her mom, it's been rough on her. I think she's glad to be going back."

"That's too bad," said Lucy. "Relationships can be hard."

"I really feel bad for her," I said.

"Having a bad day?" We all looked up from our food to see Goldie standing at the end of the booth with a smirk on her face. She grabbed a chair from a nearby table and sat with us.

"Why did you run?" I asked.

"Better question, why were you chasing me? I didn't know who you were. You might've been that nasty paparazzi." She smiled like the Cheshire cat.

"We know what you did and you're not getting away with it." I snarled.

"Get away with what?" She gave us all a sickly sweet smile and settled into her chair, setting her purse on the table. "Waitress," she called behind her. "I'll have a white wine and put it on their tab." We sat there uncomfortably not knowing what to say. This woman was dangerous and had most likely killed before.

"What do you want, Goldie," Vana finally asked as the silence dragged on.

Doris brought her wine and set it on the table before her. Goldie made a show out of swirling it and taking a sip. "I have everything I want. The question is, what do you want? How do you know your friend Audrey isn't behind all this? She's the one with all the money now. I'm just a poor grieving widow. Why are you harassing me?"

"Harassing you?" I asked.

"Yes. You've been following me all week. First at the open house and then at the movies. Why are you stalking me?"

"Stalking you? You stole Audrey's car and pretended to be her," I said.

"Is that what she told you? She was running late and asked me to open the house for her." She took another sip of wine and then picked up her purse and stood up. "Maybe, Audrey is trying to frame me so I can't contest the will. Did you ever think of that? My poor Charlie died after Velma, so that money will be mine and when I get it, I'm going to buy that house with the balcony that you were eavesdropping on me from. Oh yes, I know everything."

She picked up the wine glass and downed the remainder and then set it back gently on the table. "I suppose it's a good thing your cop friend is getting you sent home tomorrow, so you don't get into any more trouble. It can be dangerous, poking your nose where it doesn't belong."

She sauntered off slowly to the door and I rubbed my cheek where I had been biting the inside of it to keep silent hoping she would say something to incriminate herself.

We all let out a deep breath when she left.

"You don't think what she said about Audrey is true. Do you?" Asked Lucy. "She didn't strike me as dishonest."

"I think she's more dangerous than we thought and it's probably a good thing that we're going home," said Shelby. "Audrey wouldn't hurt a fly. What do you think Holly?"

They all looked at me. "Holly," questioned Vana. "You don't really believe what you said in the car do you?"

"I don't know what to think. I mean what's the chance that we would go to an open house that had a dead body in it? You picked that open house by random, didn't you?" I asked Vana who was now biting her lower lip.

"Maybe I was talking to Travis before we left and maybe he mentioned that his cousin worked here and maybe when I looked her up, I saw that she was holding an open house and mentioned it to Vana," admitted Shelby. "I'm sorry."

"You've been lying to me this whole time? How could you? Is that what's been going on between the two of you?"

"Hey," interjected Vana, "she just mentioned the open house. I didn't know anything about Audrey being Travis's cousin." She put her hand on my arm and I brushed it off and stood up.

"You know what Shelby, maybe you should find your own way home. I don't think I want to travel with someone who's so deceitful. I'm done with the whole thing. You guys can solve this mystery yourself."

I grabbed my purse and walked out the door. The beach house really wasn't that far from the restaurant so I took off my shoes and walked along the shore. I guess that's how that saying came about, "with friends like these, who needs enemies."

I knew something was up with Shelby. She'd been acting weird the entire time we'd been there. Was that why Travis really came? Because she was trying to set me up with him and figured a mystery would clinch it?

Except that, there really had been a dead body and Nick seemed like a kid that was really suffering. If there was anyone innocent in this it was him. And Velma. She certainly had nothing to do with this. All she wanted to do was find her kid and she hadn't even gotten to do that. I laughed to myself at my next thought. She must have been a nice person if Bob liked her. Animals tend to have a good sense of people. So what did that say about me?

I'd just yelled at my best friends who always have my back. Is that Goldie's real talent? Making people turn against each other? Calvin's wife sure wanted to kill her. Which got me thinking, was it only because she stole her husband and planted evidence against her? Most women wouldn't turn their stepson into a killer unless they were a little off to begin with. Maybe like Bob, she recognized a dangerous woman when she saw one.

Which meant that Audrey was innocent and Goldie was trying to set her up too. I couldn't let that happen. I had some serious apologizing to do. I pulled out my phone and composed several texts and then hurried back to the beach house.

I had the ride share drop me off a block from Charlie's house. I wanted the truth from Goldie and she wasn't going to spill it if others were with me.

The streetlights were on and the streets were empty when I pulled up in her driveway. I could see why she was jealous of Velma and her money. The house was tiny and located on a residential street with other tiny houses with small front yards.

She answered my knock dressed in red velvet sweats. She looked me up and down with a condescending look on her face.

"What do you want?"

"You're right. I just want to clear the air. Can I come in?"

She glanced around outside and then opened the door all the way. "Sure, why not."

I followed her inside and pressed send on my phone in my jacket pocket. The room had expensive leather furniture and quality end tables. The drapes were modern and the kitchen, from what I could see through the kitchen door, had top of the line appliances. Aside from that, it was dark and boring. Which answered one question for me, Charlie had never been the target, it had been Velma's money all along.

"It's never been about the men, has it?" I asked, still standing in the hall. Goldie barely glanced at me as she moved over to the liquor cabinet in the corner of the living room.

"I like nice things, and why shouldn't I have them?" Ice clinked into a glass and then she poured alcohol from a crystal decanter over the top of them. She turned and said "cheers." We stood across the room from each other, neither willing to sit before the other.

"You want what you can't have. It's all about the game and the money is just the icing on top. What happened to Velma?"

Goldie smiled and then finally crossed over to the couch to sit, crossing her right leg over her left knee. "She was smart. Too smart. She researched everything and questioned me about her treatment. She was also selfless to a fault. I could see my way to her money was through Charlie. She encouraged him to date me. It was so perfect. All I had to do was wait for her to pass."

I crossed to the chair nearest me and sat on the edge. "How long have you been seeing the lawyer? Nice touch setting up the wife."

"Oh, you know about that do you?"

"It had to have been a while. You needed access to her photos, that might take a while to find. I'll admit, it really confused me why you went after him after going to all that work to make it look like Charlie died after Velma. But then I realized you had already moved on from Charlie weeks ago. That's why his wife tried to have her son kill you at the movies."

Goldie laughed. "That's not her son, it's his son. Once he asked for a divorce, she threatened to, destroy us." There was just the slightest hesitation between those last two words, but I caught it. She really was crafty and was going to change the story to benefit her. "Once Audrey is convicted of Charlie's death, all that money will come to me. You have no proof, I've done anything wrong."

I finally put the last puzzle piece in place and smiled at her. "Except."

"Except what?"

"You made a mistake."

"And what would that be darling?" She looked at me with the smuggest look on her face. I wanted to slap it off.

"Charlie had a head injury when he died. What happened? Did Charlie find out you were dating the lawyer and confront you? Did you push him and cause him to have a heart attack?" I was totally guessing on this part, but it sounded plausible. "I can't believe you just stood by and watched him die and then stuffed him in the closet but I'm guessing this is all old hat for you."

I stopped talking. Goldie was staring at me, chewing on the inside of her cheek. She was nervous and I was missing something.

"You're treading on thin ice. Maybe you should go before something happens to you," she said calmly, arching one eyebrow for dramatic effect.

As I watched her reaction I knew I had hit the proverbial nail on the head. Unfortunately, as she said, there was no way to prove anything.

"You go right ahead and take that to the police and see where it gets you," she said smugly.

I stood up. "You're right I can't. But I will make sure that Audrey doesn't get charged with anything and then you'll never get the money." As I reached the front door, Goldie's glass came flying past me to hit the door frame and shatter into a thousand pieces. Without turning, I said, "You have a good night Goldie," then I left the house.

Once I was safely down the street and in my ride share, I picked up my phone with shaking hands and nearly dropped it back on the floor. "Did you get all that?" After receiving an affirmative, I hung up.

I entered the living room of the beach house to find six pairs of eyes staring at me. Travis, Scott, Audrey, Lucy, Shelby and Vana all stared at me with varying degrees of anger and frustration on their faces. Apparently, Scott had shared the phone recording with them.

Scott had been the easy choice, although, if he hadn't still been in town, I would have called Travis whether he liked it or not. I wasn't stupid. I held up a hand to stave off their questions. "First I just want to apologize to all of you. I trust you and I know that none of you would do anything to ever hurt me. I know I shouldn't have gone alone, but I had to make one last try." After a few moments of silence I asked, "so now what do we do about Goldie?"

Travis spoke first. "Even with the accusation of assault against Charlie, there's no evidence so the district attorney is refusing to press charges." Good, at least he wasn't yelling at me.

"Bu...but she killed someone. She moved a dead body and, and she drove on the beach," said Lucy.

"We don't have any proof of any of that and Vana also drove on the beach, erratically and drove into the surf. If they charge Goldie, they'll have to charge Vana. You don't want that do you?" He asked.

"No. I guess not. What about her son?"

"We tried, he won't talk."

"What about the lawyer's son?" I said.

Travis and Scott both shook their heads. "We're working on it, but as you said, daddy is a lawyer," said Scott.

"So we have nothing?" I cried in frustration. The two men glanced at each other before answering.

"Sorry," said Travis.

"The coroner is running tests on the two bodies and if there's anything there to suggest foul play, then we will have her arrested. In the meantime, we are keeping her under surveillance. It's the best we can do," said Scott. He looked tired and frustrated and mirrored what we were all feeling. I knew in my gut she was guilty and I wasn't going to let her frame an innocent person.

"Do we still have to leave tomorrow?" I asked Travis.

He grimaced, "Yes. I did my best, but I could only get you the 24 hours."

I smiled at him. "Yes you did. Thank you. And thank you for keeping us out of jail. That wouldn't have gone well for my real estate license."

"You're welcome and if you do anything stupid like you did tonight by yourself, I will throw you in jail myself."

"I'm so sorry, you weren't able to find the will." Audrey looked dejected. She clasped both my hands in hers. "Thank you for everything you did for me. I hope that some day it will turn up." She said the words but there wasn't any hope on her face. It's so hard to accept defeat sometimes.

"Thank you for all of your hospitality. You never know, maybe the child will come looking for their mother." That thought made me even sadder. Finally discovering who your mother is, just to learn they have passed away. How horrible.

"And, you, please come back and visit me sometime. I know a wonderful little tea house we can go to. Are you sure you don't want me to take you tomorrow?"

"No, sense in you having to drive all that way to the airport," I said.

"Well anyway, I'm over in the morning to say goodbye." I gave her a hug and Travis, Scott and Audrey all left the house. We made sure everything was locked up tight and I went to bed frustrated at my lack of ability to solve this case.

The next morning the ride share pulled up to the curb and honked at us. We all gave Audrey a quick hug while Travis piled our suitcases in the trunk. Shelby stood in the drive hanging onto her case.

"Shelby come on," said Lucy. "We've got to go."

She shook her head, as if she had come to a decision. "I'm not going."

"What?" we all said.

"I'm actually going to meet up with a friend and I'll catch a flight home in a few days. Lucy, Vana and I all gave her our concerned mom looks.

"I'll be fine. I promise," she said. "It's just a couple days. Come on, can't a girl have a little fun?"

"What's your friend's name?"

"Michaela Larkin," she answered immediately and put us more at ease.

Lucy frowned at her, "are you sure?"

Shelby shrugged her shoulders, "yeah. The cops said we had to leave town, they didn't say we couldn't go up the coast to another town."

"Okay, but you better be home in a couple days,"

"Okay, mom." Shelby drew out the last word mockingly.

"Okay then, have a fantastic time for us." We all gave her a hug as another ride share pulled up and she got inside, waving good bye to us.

"I hope she has a good time," said Travis, who was returning to Appleby with us. Probably to make sure we actually went home.

The Hindu driver, who had waited a bit impatiently for us, pulled away from the curb. It was bitter sweet that we had to leave Audrey behind to solve the mystery of the missing child herself. At least we could come back for tea sometime after the police forgot about us.

"Wait! Stop the car!" I yelled. The driver let out a sigh and stepped on the brake.

"What's going on? Holly, we're going to miss our flight," said Vana. She was a little bitter that she wasn't driving.

Instead of answering, I jumped out of the car and ran back up to Audrey, who was standing there

"Didn't you say, Velma came over to visit you before you left?" Audrey nodded in confusion. "Did you check your coat pockets?

Where would you hide a will you wanted to be found but so it would be protected?"

By this time the rest of the girls had followed me. "In a friend's jacket," they all yelled. We returned to the car and redirected the driver to Audrey's house.

"No."

"No?"

"I can't just change the route, there's rules."

"We'll pay whatever you need."

"It's not that. I was contracted to take you to the airport and I must take you there unless you cancel the ride." He sat in the driver's seat with his arms crossed.

"Oh, for heaven's sake," cried Lucy. "She pulled out her phone and opened the rideshare app. "There, a new request to go to Audrey's house. Can we go now?"

"Of course," he said. "As soon as you cancel the previous request. There will be a cancellation charge." We all rolled our eyes as Lucy grabbed Vana's phone.

"What? It was on your phone," she said.

"Oh for the love of Pete," hissed Vana as she canceled the original request. Finally, he started the car and we got underway.

"Can I ask you a question?" he asked, looking in the rearview mirror.

"Yes, what?" I replied.

"Why did you not just go in your friend's car?"

"Because we didn't...Oh, never mind. Can you drive faster please?"

He smiled politely, "I cannot. There are speed limits for a reason."

We resigned ourselves to arriving at the designated time and not a minute sooner.

Upon arrival at Audrey's, Travis grabbed the suitcases from the trunk as we all piled out of the car and up the front steps to Audrey's house. She had beaten us by five minutes because our driver would not exceed the speed limit, no matter how much we begged.

"This way ladies," she said, directing us to her bedroom and the large walk in closet.

"Oh, nice," admired Lucy as she stopped in the doorway to the closet. "This is really a nice size."

"Would you get out of the way," I yelled.

"Oops, sorry. It's not often I get to see..."

"Lucy!"

"Fine." She moved out of the way and we all took a section of the closet and started searching pockets. I was the lucky one and my hand closed over a piece of paper in the pocket of a cute sundress, yellow with little orange sunflowers.

"Yes!" I yelled, holding it up.

"That's a receipt," said Vana dourly.

"Oh, well that's disappointing. The dress is cute though, right?" They all glared at me and we went back to searching.

"I, um," Audrey cleared her voice. "I think I found it." She held a thick business envelope in her hand. "It was in a coat she gave me for my birthday two years ago."

"Maybe we should all go to the kitchen to look at it," Lucy suggested. "I'll make some tea." Without speaking, we all retired to the kitchen, walking past the living room, where Travis was sitting on the couch. We stopped and stared at him.

"What?" he said. "I figured I'd leave you all to it. I'm sure you're better at searching pockets than I would be."

I wanted to make a smart remark, but the fact was, we hadn't even noticed he wasn't there. Instead we continued on and sat down at the table where Audrey laid the envelope down in front of us all.

She put her hands in her lap as she looked at it. "I don't think I can open it. One of you do it."

"I think I'm too nervous," said Lucy. "Holly, you do it."

"Travis!" I yelled. "Get in here and open this envelope." He walked through the kitchen doorway to find us all staring at him.

"What envelope?"

"The will," I said.

"You found the will?"

"Open it!" we all yelled out in frustration.

He picked up the envelope from the table and flipped it over in his hands. "You could have at least let me know you found it," he remarked. At this point I think he was beginning to feel the heat from our glares and he slipped a finger under the flap and slid it open.

Unfolding the enclosed paper, Travis took a moment to look it over. We were all antsy with anticipation. "Are you gonna read it?" I asked quietly.

"Uh, yeah," he said. "But it's not a will."

September 15, 2024

Audrey, I want you to know that you were right when you told me so long ago to give my child a chance by giving her up to better parents. I have reached out to the adoption agency in the hope that I might find her before I die. Unfortunately, it doesn't look as if this will happen. I trust you and I know that you will do what is best for her when you either find her, or she finds you.

"I give you complete control of my trust because I know you will do the right thing with the money. When you do find her, please give her my diary. Maybe it will bring her some solace. The agency told me that she has had a good life, a life that wouldn't have been possible with me.

"One more thing, please protect Nick and Charlie. I worry about them. Perhaps you can help Nick go away to school and get away from her. I wanted to leave him something but I'm afraid he would never receive it. Look out for him, he's like a son to me.

Always remember, friends can be found everywhere. Even cranky ones.

Always your friend,

Velma

VANA WIPED A TEAR FROM her eye. "That's so sad."

"I know, right?" agreed Lucy, also wiping her eyes.

Where was the other envelope? "We have to go back to the lawyer's," I declared.

"We have to leave town," pointed out Travis politely.

"You said tomorrow. Today is tomorrow all the way up until midnight," I pointed out to him, equally as politely. He sighed and hung his head.

Lucy raised her eyebrows at me. "Too bad Shelby is missing out on this."

"Yes, so much excitement," said Vana sarcastically.

This time we did take Audrey's car to Calvin Tremont's, who was fortunately still in his office. We dashed in past the secretary to confront him.

"Mr. Tremont, we only found a letter, there was no will and no second envelope with a name. Can't you tell us what was in the will?" I asked.

"I wish I could, " he shook his head sadly. "I unfortunately cannot without the will it would only be supposition."

"And there were no other copies made?"

"No. Just the one in my file and the one Velma took."

"Is it unusual for people to do that?" Calvin's chair creaked as he leaned back and folded his hands over his chest. "People can be weird when it comes to wills. I don't know what else I can tell you. I already told you client confidentiality precludes me telling you anything else."

"We just have one question. Did you actually see her put the letter in the envelope and seal it?"

"That I can answer. No, I did not. I gave her privacy and she walked out with the envelope in her hand. She gave the sealed envelope to me and I notarized it. But like I told you already, the actual will is gone."

Smiling graciously, I replied, "Thank you for your time." I reached out and shook his hand and we all left. I could see the questions on their faces but I waited until we were back in the car to answer.

"I don't think there ever was a second envelope. Just as I don't believe there was an actual will."

"What are you saying," asked Audrey. "Why would he lie to us?"

I turned to her, thinking while I was speaking, which caused my words to come out disjointed. "I don't think she made one because she already had the trust with the funds from the house going to it, leaving it all to you." I tapped my lips with my finger tips. "What did she do with her family money?"

"What?" said Audrey at the sudden switch.

"When we first met, you said she had family money and that's how she could afford not working. What happens to that money?"

Audrey clasped her hands to her chest. "I, I don't know. I just assumed it would be in the will." She looked dejected. "Calvin won't tell us anything."

"How sure are we that he isn't in on it?" Asked Lucy. "It's only his word that Goldie stole his copy."

I stared at her and slowly said, "but he didn't say that, we did. He said it was 'gone.' That could mean different things."

"So is there a will or isn't there?" snapped Lucy.

"Wow! Cranky much?" commented Vana in a snarky tone.

"It isn't the will we need as much as the envelope with the name inside." I said. "I think she found her kid and wrote their name in the envelope. Goldie admitted she showed Charlie the will. What if Velma figured it out and was trying to protect her child from Goldie. Goldie said she was smart. Maybe the will was a decoy."

"Why wouldn't she have told me?" asked Audrey.

"If she was afraid of Goldie, maybe she was worried about you as well." I was thinking. "Maybe it's best if we don't find the kid. At least they're safe now, wherever they are."

"Perhaps you're right," said Audrey. She looked miserable. The letter had done little to console her. Velma was gone. Charlie was gone. There was no way Goldie could get the money now that she had basically admitted to pushing Charlie and watching him die. Okay, she didn't admit it, but she didn't deny it either. In my book that screams guilty. I guess sometimes you don't get satisfaction.

"We should probably go," said Travis. "We've missed our flight but I called in some favors and got the tickets exchanged for 7 pm tonight."

"What do you mean we're leaving? We can't leave now," whined Lucy. "We haven't found the diary."

"I'm sorry Lucy, we have to go back, we have work waiting for us. Georgie is probably getting lonely. Sometimes we don't get all the answers." Even as I said the words, I didn't believe them. I'd never felt so frustrated in my life."

"But that poor kid. There's millions waiting for them, it could change their life," said Lucy despondently. I agreed, it was terrible, but what could we do? We'd looked everywhere. Clearly Goldie didn't have it. Although it would fit her personality to keep it from us.

"Once escrow closes, I'm going to hire a private investigator to track down Velma's child," declared Audrey.

Travis patted her on the shoulder, "maybe that will make it easier to find them."

"Oh, I do hope so."

"You know what?" said Vana suddenly, "let's go do something fun. Today is Tiffany's last day at the restaurant. I know I'm hungry."

"You're always hungry," retorted Lucy. "But yeah, let's go do that."

Audrey was very quiet in the car ride over, while everyone else was babbling. "Cat got your tongue, Audrey?" I asked.

She looked very serious as if she was trying to remember something. "It's just that, I swear I wore that coat not two weeks ago and that letter wasn't in there then."

"Are you sure? I know sometimes, I have a difficult time remembering things exactly."

She gave a brief smile and patted my leg, "Perhaps you're right. Is that your way of calling me old?"

I laughed at her. "Look, you still have your sense of humor."

THE RESTAURANT ONLY held a few tables of patrons at this time of the day and so we selected seats at a table next to the huge picture window. It would be our last view of the sunshine and ocean. Tiffany saw us and came over to say good bye. "Hi ladies, I'm actually on my way out. I just came to get my last check."

"We know," said Vana, "that's why we came by. Can you sit down and eat dinner with us?"

At her hesitation, we all joined in to convince her and she finally gave in and sat down with us. "You deserve to be a customer at least once," said Lucy.

"So tell us what happened with your mom, if you don't mind," said Vana. She could get a rock to talk. Tiffany chewed on her bottom lip and looked sad.

"I never found her. She sent me this letter with her address and phone number but I never got an answer. I've been here a month already. She was never home and didn't answer her phone."

"Oh, I'm so sorry to hear that," said Vana. "Well, let's just enjoy a good dinner. It must be strange to eat here and have someone else serve you."

With the conversation on another track, we enjoyed good food and company along with laughs as they regaled Tiffany with my adventures at the beach. As they talked my mind kept wandering back over the facts. Something had been bothering me this whole time and I couldn't put my finger on it.

I had seen something that was relevant but I didn't know what it was. Goldie began dating the lawyer a month ago. Why at that particular time? Velma had been sick for the eight months previous. Why that time? Was it because Velma had created a trust for the house? Except, I didn't think Goldie knew about that. So what? She sat there at our table smug knowing something that we didn't.

Why would Velma suddenly create a trust and change her will one month ago? Out the window I could just make out the lights on the harbor around the bend and wondered who Bob was harassing tonight. Now Tiffany was laughing at Lucy's description of me flying through the air after the dog knocked me off the porch. Travis seemed to be having a good time also, although he kept glancing at his phone.

Maybe Audrey could hire her, if she wanted to come stay. Paperwork would be much easier than waitressing. Tiffany. She'd been here a month also. That's when all the pieces suddenly fell into place.

"Audrey," I said a bit too loudly. "Who does Tiffany remind you of?" The conversation ceased and everyone looked at me. "When you first saw Tiffany, you said she looked familiar."

"Yes, I did, I. She reminds me of Velma. It must be because she's been on my mind lately. I keep seeing her everywhere."

"Or it's because she's Velma's daughter." I let the statement sink in for a few moments before continuing on. They all looked at me like I was bonkers. "Think about it," I said. "One month ago, Tiffany arrives. One month ago, Velma creates a trust. One month ago Goldie started dating the lawyer and stole the will." I looked each person in the eyes before delivering my pièce de résistance. "One month ago, a girl was killed in this parking lot by a hit and run driver. Goldie was so smug, when she was taunting us here. Why was she be so confident that she would get the money. Why the ruse to show that Charlie died first? Why? Because she knew Velma's daughter was dead. Or she thought she was."

I shook my head. "She killed the wrong girl."

"How, how can you know that?" questioned Audrey.

"Goldie told me Velma was smart. I think she made a fake will to protect Charlie and her daughter. Somehow she discovered what Goldie was up to." I slammed my hand on the table. "If only we could find that diary."

Tiffany's face was pale and full of doubt. "Bu, but my mom's name is Ellen," she whispered.

Audrey's eyes glistened as she reached out a hand to Tiffany's. "Velma's middle name is Ellen.

"I don't understand," said Tiffany, "you know my mom?"

I looked at her sadly, "No. We don't but Audrey did."

Tears appeared in her eyes, "What do you mean, did?"

I took her hand in mine. When you had to deliver bad news, sometimes a human touch made it easier. "I'm sorry to tell you this, but your mom passed away a few days ago. She had cancer. I'm sorry."

"But I've been here for a month. Why didn't she call me back?"

That was a very good question. Why didn't Velma get Tiffany's messages? "Audrey?" I asked, directing the question to her.

"I, I don't know. She had her phone with her the whole time. She wasn't home, she was in convalescence on hospice care. The stairs at home were too much for her."

Suddenly the pieces all clicked in my brain. "Goldie tried to kill you," I said solemnly.

"What?" came from five voices at once. And so I explained.

"Goldie found out about the child. Somehow she must have found the envelope. Goldie had access to the house through Charlie and she must have cloned Velma's phone in case she made contact. She deleted the messages so Velma wouldn't know Tiffany was in town."

"To what purpose?" asked Lucy.

"To keep them apart. Accidents happen all the time. If there's no surviving heir, Charlie would inherit and then in turn, Goldie," I explained.

Audrey covered her mouth. "Oh, that's so awful. Tiffany could have met her mother and Goldie took that away."

I didn't say what I really thought, that Goldie was a psychopath and enjoyed ruining people's lives. Nobody needed to hear that right now. Instead I offered Tiffany some hope.

"Velma, Vickie, left behind a diary. I don't believe Goldie ever found it. I'm hoping it will still turn up. Your mom wanted you to have it. Until then, Audrey here is your mom's oldest and dearest friend and I'm sure she can tell you anything you want to know about her."

"Of course, I will," agreed Audrey. "Anything you need. And if you don't want to leave right away, you can come stay with me. Escrow doesn't close on your mom's place for a few weeks. You can help me pack it up and I'll tell you about her while we do it. That's if you want to." She looked at Tiffany hopefully. I think she needed this time for closure, as much as Tiffany did.

Tiffany nodded her head in agreement, her eyes brimming with tears.

"Oh, and you're rich," added Lucy. "Not that that's the important thing right now," she added after I glared at her. What's money, when you've just lost the mom you never met. If I ever get the chance, I'm going to make Goldie pay for taking that moment away from Tiffany.

"Where's Travis?" I asked, suddenly realizing he was gone.

"Oh he stepped away a few minutes ago," said Vana. "Probably went to the bathroom."

"I'm sure he'll be back soon. But he didn't come back. We were nearly done eating when I finally got a text from him. "I had to check on a hunch. I'll see you soon." Well, that was pretty cryptic. What hunch? I ordered him a turkey sandwich to go and texted back that I'd see him at the house.

Vana waited until we were all back in the car with our seatbelts on before clearing her throat. "Before we leave, I've got one more open house to go to," said Vana. We all groaned. "Come on, it's just one and I really want you to see it. It won't take but five minutes. I promise. And we're not leaving until seven tonight anyway."

"Fine." I said it more just to get it over with. "Oh, oh, I forgot my purse," I exclaimed and clambered back out of the car to retrieve it from the restaurant. One of the workers was grabbing a delivery order at the counter. There it was, my purse still sitting on the chair. As I grabbed it, I heard the delivery girl say, "Who eats anchovy and mushroom pizza? Yuck," said the delivery girl. I stopped short with my hand on the door. Funny, I knew a person who did just exactly that. Out of curiosity, I looked back to see her talking to Doris. It took me a $20 tip but Doris gave me the address which just happened to be a motel. I tucked the paper in my purse and walked back out to the girls. The whole experience triggered something in my brain but as usual the memory wouldn't come to me.

LAST OPEN HOUSE

Vana's final open house turned out to be in a nice neighborhood, blocks from the beach on a hill with a great view. That was the last nice thing about it. The yard was overgrown and most of the plants were dead. Paint was peeling off everything on the outside of the house.

"Wow. This house is just creepy. It looks like it hasn't been updated since it was built," commented Lucy. We all kind of huddled away from the walls because it was so dirty, we didn't want to touch anything.

It was dark, dark paneling, dark drapes, dark wood furniture. The layout was okay though. If a couple walls were opened up and everything was painted in light colors, it might actually be pretty nice. It had large windows and high ceilings. Vana threw open the drapes and the view outside was absolutely stunning. If it was upgraded, it would be on a par with the really nice second house we saw.

"It's how much?" I gasped when she told us the price. "Isn't that kind of cheap for this area?"

"This looks like a murder house," commented Lucy. "Good thing Shelby's not here to see it.

"It is."

"Yeah, I totally get that vibe," Audrey said oblivious to Vana's statement.

"No seriously, someone was murdered here. That's why it's so cheap."

"And why are we here?" I asked, shocked. Some people go in for those cheap thrills but I wasn't one of them.

"I'm thinking of buying it." We all looked at her as you would someone who was out of their mind. Lucy put her hand on Vana's forehead.

"Nope, no fever." Vana slapped her hand away.

"It's under market and Bob and I have always wanted a house by the beach."

We looked at her dumbfounded. "But somebody died here."

People die in houses all the time," she said blithely.

"Not violently," Lucy and I said at the same time.

"Maybe not, but they're not here now," she replied. She always was the practical one. "Hey, Holly, did you ever find any information on that finger bone you found in Carol's garage?"

"What?"

"This house made me think of that, you know skeletons in the closet,"

"Yeah, way to make a person feel better," remarked Lucy.

"No. I haven't actually checked into it or the missing treasure. I wasn't going to,"

"No. But now that you're a sleuth don't you think you should?"

"You are just trying to change the subject. Has Bob actually seen this place?"

"Yeah, it was his idea. We're not afraid of no ghosts."

"Is it haunted?" Lucy shrieked.

I pinched the bridge of my nose, thinking. Taking my hand down, I confronted Vana. "That's why you took us to the first house isn't it? So this one wouldn't look so bad."

Vana threw her hands in the air. "You got me. I didn't know there was going to be a dead body though, I swear."

I laughed. "Fix this up and it will look great and maybe we'll forget about the murders."

Lucy and Audrey looked at me like I had lost my marbles. "I won't," they said together.

My phone rang and we all screamed. I fished it out of my purse, "it's Travis. Hey Travis what's up?"

"Is Audrey still with you?"

"Yeah, why?"

"Have her bring you down to the police station."

"Okay, why..." but he had already disconnected the call.

INTERROGATION

We arrived at the police station where Travis met us in the lobby. He had a grin from ear to ear. "I think we got her," he said.

"Who?" I asked, puzzled.

"Goldie. She's in the interrogation room. I told her we needed a statement from her about Audrey, that we were investigating her for Charlie's death. She was more than willing to cooperate."

"I don't understand."

"When you said you thought she tried to kill Tiffany. I looked up the report. There was security footage from a neighboring business. A dark car hit the girl in the parking lot. I bet if we check, we'll find it was stolen. The good news is, a business down the road caught her in the car. The bad news is, the footage isn't very clear. They're executing a search warrant for her house right now."

He looked so happy, I hated to burst his bubble, but I did. "She'll never admit it. If she's done this before, she's going to be way too careful."

He shook his head, his mouth a thin line. "We only have to trip her up once," he said hopefully.

I watched through the one way window as she sat in the interrogation room. Travis walked back in and sat down across from her, placing a manilla folder on the table in front of him.

"What do you want to know about Audrey?" she asked with a smirk on her face. Her whole demeanor was one of confidence and arrogance.

"We're not really here about Audrey." Travis leaned forward and clasped his hands in front of him on the table top. Carter told us everything," he said looking her directly in her eyes. I had to give her credit, she never wavered.

"He told you nothing, because I haven't done anything."

Travis opened the folder and took out a picture which he flipped around and slid in front of her. "Except try to run down an innocent girl." He slid another photo over to her. "This one was taken a few moments later as you left the restaurant. We have video showing you heading towards the restaurant a few moments before the accident and leaving immediately after, which proves that you only went there to deliberately hit that poor girl. I believe you knew she was Velma's daughter."

Goldie kept her mouth shut.

Travis tilted his head at her. "Except."

"Except what?" she said with contempt on her face.

"We know you began dating the lawyer, Calvin Tremont, a month ago. Surprise, surprise, Velma's will is suddenly found missing. The only way you could have known about Tiffany, is if you found the will."

My butt got tickled and I pulled out my phone to see a text from Audrey. She sent me a picture. As soon as I read the note, I forwarded it on to Travis. I watched as he pulled out his phone annoyed and glanced at the text.

Goldie took the distraction as an opportunity to take a deep centering breath and lean forward, clasping her hands together on the table top.

"I don't think you have anything, or you would have arrested me already. In which case, I would bring suit against you for an unlawful arrest."

Wow, she was good.

Travis fiddled with his phone, said, "hmm," and then put his right elbow on the table and rested his chin on his hand. "Perhaps, there's video footage of you breaking into Audrey's house to put the letter in her jacket pocket two weeks ago. Did you remember to wear gloves?"

Goldie's eyes finally flared a little but she didn't speak.

"You seem like the type of person who takes pride in their work. I'm pretty sure you wouldn't leave this to someone else to do. Naw, that would open you up to blackmail. No. You did it yourself. Even now we have technicians going through your house and Audrey's. What do you suppose they are going to find?"

I texted a question to Travis. He barely glanced at his phone.

"One month ago, you started dating the lawyer. One month ago, Velma created a trust with her good friend Audrey as trustee. One month ago, Tiffany Hall came to town looking for her mother. One month ago, you mowed her down with your car."

Travis looked down at the table and laughed, then looked back up at Goldie. "Do you know what's funny? Carter Atley, I'll bet he'll testify it was you. Once we get the drug tests back from Velma and Charlie's bodies, I think we'll have enough evidence to convict you. Anything you want to say?"

Goldie looked down at the top of the table. I could see her eyes darting back and forth as she tried to come up with anything but the truth. She finally looked up at him.

"I don't know what you're talking about."

"Well now, here's the clincher. The baby is Charlie's isn't it? You showed him the will and the letter and he knew. That's why he was searching for the diary, he wanted to know who his child was. I think he confronted you at Velma's house just before she died and you shoved him, causing him to fall and hit his head, causing his heart attack. And then you watched him die and you did nothing to help him."

During this conversation, Goldie's face started twitching and her breathing came faster. And this was when Travis's brilliance came into play. He picked up his papers and walked to the door to leave. He stopped at the door and turned back to Goldie. Columbo couldn't have done it any better.

"Just one more thing. Did you keep the phone you cloned from Velma's? If you'd checked it, you would have known, you hit the wrong girl."

"No! There were no messages." As soon as she said it, she realized her mistake.

"Thanks Goldie. Once we get the evidence from Charlie's body, we're going to exhume all your dead husbands. I think you know what we'll find."

"He was going to change his will and leave it all to that kid." Her voice was shaking as she said it. "He still loved her," she spat out through gritted teeth. "All that work and I would get nothing. Nothing!" she screamed. All because of some meddlesome real estate agents!"

I was never more proud of him. But another part of me was sad. It had just been a hunch about Charlie being the father. I remembered Harold said they were high school sweethearts and it just made sense. Poor Tiffany had lost both parents in one weekend.

Travis came back into the observation room. "Congratulations," I said.

"I couldn't have done it without you. How did you know?"

"It was just a hunch."

"Well it was a good one. We have cause to hold her until we get the evidence we need. Clearly she's a flight risk. Good work Holly."

"Hey, mind if I borrow your car? I have something I need to do before we leave town."

"Sure, do you want me to drive you somewhere?"

"No, I need to do this on my own. But thanks for the offer." I gave him a quick hug and snuck out the back way to avoid the others waiting in the lobby.

SURPRISE

I pulled up in front of an apartment building and double checked the address on the piece of paper I'd gotten from Doris. I gave a quick tap on the door, not that I knew what I was going to do if anyone answered. As I knocked the door moved inward a tiny bit. Apparently, it hadn't been closed all the way.

I pushed a little harder and waited. When no one responded, I ducked my head through the doorway and looked inside. This room was a suite and was quite empty. There were voices coming from what I supposed was the bedroom.

I crossed the room silently on the plush carpet, listening to the conversation. The more I heard, the more puzzled I became.

I pushed the bedroom door open all the way until it hit the wall. "Shelby, what's going on here?" I confronted her.

Sitting on the bed and using the headboard as a backrest, she was cuddled up with Carter. Her eyes widened to the size of saucers at my voice. "What are you doing here? I pulled out my phone and prepared to dial 9-1-1.

"Holly, wait! It's not what you think." She dropped her hands to her side, "please, just let me explain." With a deep sigh, She began. "Holly, I'd like you to meet my husband Michael Tranby. We're both agents with the CIA. Goldie has been traveling around the world, using her husbands' life insurance to fuel her lifestyle. She's a black widow of the worst kind because she just does it for fun."

My brain was spinning and I didn't know where to begin first. "He's your husband? But you're the most man hungry guy I've ever met?

She let out a huge sigh. "That's really your first question?" I shrugged my shoulders and tried to look contrite.

Glancing at Carter, she explained. "It's just a cover story. You would never really believe I was married would you with behavior like that?" I had to admit she was right and it was a good cover. No, actually it was a great cover. She could meet any man she wanted and no one would ever suspect because it was just Shelby, being Shelby.

"So there's no Dixie?" Dixie was her daughter, or so I thought.

She shook her head. "No, Dixie and her issues are real. Unfortunately."

"I don't get it. What are you doing in Appleby. And what is real? Have you been lying to me my whole life? I mean, we went to school together."

"I have to live somewhere. After I got divorced, I was lost and needed a change. I met Michael and he convinced me to join the firm. We've been together ever since." She looked at Michael as she said it and he gave her shoulders a comforting squeeze.

"Does Travis know?" I gasped out.

"No," interjected Michael, but Scott Williams works with me." He kissed Shelby's forehead. "Shelby convinced me to send him up to help out. She didn't want her best friend getting hurt."

A sudden thought came to me. "Omg, you saw him moving the body from the house didn't you? You've known all along. That's why you were acting so weird."

She puckered her lips and nodded her head. "I may have helped him move it," she grimaced.

I crossed my arms across my chest in an attempt to keep my anger in check.

"How did you know it was him?"

"I caught a glimpse of his red shirt outside. I gave it to him for Christmas. I knew he was here on an investigation and I just put two and two together." I had to give her credit, she knew it was him and helped him and then lied to us for the duration.

"Oh my...you did send the text! You brat! We were so worried," I yelled at her. "What were you thinking? And just...why?"

"Look, you can't tell anyone," began Carter. "This isn't the first death Goldie is suspected of. She's left a long list of deaths and pseudonyms behind her. One of whom was my boss."

I crossed to the chair in front of the window and sat down. This was a lot to take in. My lifelong friend is happily married and has been lying to me her whole life.

Shelby came over to me and knelt next to the chair. "You can't tell anyone. Ever. You actually really need to leave right now before anyone sees you. I shouldn't be here either." I looked at Shelby, really looked at her and I could see the worry and sadness reflected in her face.

When she spoke again it was in a low quiet voice. "Mike's been undercover for over a year. I just missed him so much," her voice broke.

"That's why you've been so on edge lately," I said, her behaviour finally making sense.

"How did you know?"

"It was the shirt Carter, Mike, wore on the dock, tiny fish and trees that looked like mushrooms. Fish and Fungi."

She rolled her eyes and glared at him. "I thought the menopause excuse was pretty good," she looked at me with one eyebrow raised.

"Yeah, it definitely worked. Okay, fine. My lips are sealed. But it's not my fault if the girls suddenly think you're..." I twirled my finger by my head for the universal crazy symbol. "But seriously, anchovy and mushroom pizza? You should be locked up just for that."

Shelby grabbed my hand pulling me to my feet and then shoved me toward the door. "Get out and stay out. Remember, not a peep or I'll have to kill you."

"I'll remember. You're just kidding about the killing part right?" I asked as she shut the door in my face.

Suddenly things made sense now. "Oh karate. So that's how you took down the guy in the bar. It was CIA training."

"Wait, what now?" asked Michael.

"I'll explain it later, honey."

I looked from Shelby to Carter, I mean Mike. They were clearly in love and I could only imagine how much they must miss each other. Who am I to come between love?

"I'm so sorry, Shelby. I understand I will most definitely keep your secret.

"Great! Now you have to go because I have a flight home to catch tomorrow."

"And I'm looking forward to having so much fun with your 'menopause.'" I put my fingers up in quotes when I said that. Shelby's eyes widened in alarm as I stepped through the door and closed it behind me.

Leaning against the closed door, I thought, 'yup, definitely gonna have fun with her.'

THIRD TIME'S THE CHARM

It was nearly six o'clock by the time I left Shelby. The sun had set and the harbor lights were blinking in the distance as I rounded the curve back to the precinct. As soon as I got back, we would make our third trip to the airport to leave.

I felt so bad leaving Tiffany and Audrey. A DNA test would confirm that she was Velma's daughter but what consolation would that be?

Both her parents were gone in one tragic weekend. I suppose it wasn't much different than if they had died in a car accident, but the fact that she had been there for a month and the opportunity had been lost due to deviousness made the bile rise in my stomach.

That phrase popped in my head again, "with friends like these." Why did I keep focusing on that? It was like that question, would you rather be in the woods with a bear or a strange man? I could do one better. What's worse? A psycho or a cranky sea lion?

And just like that, I knew where the diary was. Was I going alone to get it? Yes I was. I stopped at the market and bought some fresh fish, then headed toward the harbor, hoping I wasn't about to die.

FOUND

I took the fish out of its packaging and placed it back in the grocery bag. I wanted to make sure it was easy to access. If I was really lucky, I wouldn't even run into ole Bob.

I wasn't lucky.

It's really hard to listen for a sea lion when there are so many other sounds on a dock. The water slapping against the boats, horns in the distance, people's voices. Keeping my eyes peeled for Bob, I made my way down the docks to the *Velma*. It sat in its berth silent and dark. I walked as softly as I could as I made my way through the semi darkness listening for the sea lion.

What kind of a sound does a sea lion make anyway? Does it slither? Do snakes make noise? They slither. My heart did a pitter pat as I recalled the bite mark in the surfboard. I've read that sea lions can be really vicious. Why did I come here alone again?

I jumped at a noise from the boat behind me, my heart racing. The end of the pier was empty on all three sides. I guess Bob had called dibs on it. Seeing nothing, I went back to the *Velma* and left one of the fish. If nothing else, maybe I would hear Bob when he ate it.

With the light on my phone, I scanned the empty water and hoped it remained that way. I set the bag of fish on the dock and laid down on my belly to scan the supports on the dock. I finally located what I wanted on the post that was one from the end. A thin cable wound its way around the post and into the water. Taking another quick look around, I set my phone on the dock and leaned over the side and began pulling the cable up.

Whatever was on the end of it was pretty heavy, but I managed to lift it slowly. I guess I forgot to keep watch or sea lions are like ninjas but let me tell you, when one barks in your ear, you jump. Unfortunately, with my upper body suspended over the water, my jump merely landed me in the water. Instinctively I reached my hand back in a failed attempt to stop my fall but merely succeeded in knocking my phone into the water.

I know because I watched the light on it fade into the darkness. Somehow, landing in the water and not knowing where Bob was, made the ocean darker. Do I swim away? Would he come after me? Everyone tells you what to do if a bear or a lion comes after you. No one gives you tips on sea lions.

I was shivering, but not from the cold. Grasping the top of the dock, I chanced a quick peek. Bob's head was in the bag and he was devouring the fish. Now was my chance. If I got out quick enough, I could get past him and run. How fast can a sea lion go? But, the diary was possibly right there. I had to get it. So I did the stupid thing and wrapped my legs around the post and pulled the cable up.

No sea lion, however cranky, was going to keep me from giving Tiffany some closure. My hands finally closed around plastic and with a big heave, I plopped it on the dock. I was freezing, my hands were stiff and I had to figure out some way to get out of the water. There had to be some stairs right? A ladder or something.

Instead I screamed involuntarily when something touched my face. The something turned out to be a hand attached to an arm which belonged to none other than Ahab himself. He pulled me out and wrapped a blanket around me.

"Th th thank yu you," I managed to stutter as water puddled around my feet.

"Next time you might want to make friends with Bob first before you go swimming." His eyes landed on the dark blob on the dock. Tipping his chin at it, he asked, "what did you find?"

Shivering as I was, I was in no condition to stop him as he knelt beside the plastic box and opened. Rising, he turned to me with a grim look on his face.

"I see you've found Velma's diary. I'm afraid I'm going to need that."

My heart sank at his words.

"I suspect it's going to be useful at Goldie's trial." My eyes opened wide as he illuminated his face with a flashlight and then reached up and pulled off the mustache and beard.

"Scott?" I exclaimed in shock.

"Yeah, I've been undercover here with Carter since Goldie came to town. Never suspected Velma might have left her diary with Bob for safe keeping. Smart girl."

"You nearly gave me a heart attack," I said.

Scott laughed. "Travis called me and told me they arrested her. Hopefully, this has the information we really need to put her away for a long time."

"Why would you think that?" I asked.

"Velma. She's an old friend of the family. She got suspicious after Goldie suggested certain treatments. That's when I ran into Carter he'd been following her off and on since her third husband died, which also happened to be his boss."

"He told me."

"I should probably get you back to the precinct. I'm pretty sure you just missed your flight."

"And maybe you could call Travis for me. My phone is currently at the bottom of the harbor."

Once I was safely ensconced in Scott's warm car, I asked the burning question that had been bothering me. "How did you know that Bob liked Velma? How long have you been here?"

"Those are two very good questions. That's why Shelby recommended you. First, I've been out here for eight months. Velma contacted the FBI after she got sick and Charlie began dating Goldie. She'd become suspicious after talking with Nick about all their moving and her many husbands dying. She'd been documenting it all in her diary. How did you know where it was?"

"She left a letter for Audrey. The last line said something about cranky friends. When you called Bob a cranky sea lion, it just put it together, no ships at the end of the pier and everyone terrified of Bob. It just made sense. And what do you mean Shelby recommended me? She told me she just mentioned the open house in casual conversation with Vana? Did she set this whole thing up? Has Travis known the whole time?"

Scott made an oops face. "Shelby might have mentioned that you are good at figuring things out plus I was there for the Fall Festival and you were great at that."

Now that I was warm, the fatigue hit me and a yawn cracked my jaws. Despite the sudden tiredness my mind was still working out details. "She set up the whole thing, with Lucy getting the beach house and everything." It wasn't a question. "I'm going to kill her."

"I'd appreciate it if you didn't," he said with a laugh. "She's actually a really good agent. Yes, I know you talked to her."

"So you're CIA or FBI?"

"FBI. Because Goldie's spouses died in different states we could investigate and I've collaborated with local police and Michael before."

The whole thing just kept getting better and better. Is that really why Travis came? His investigation. Shelby and Vana sharing a secret and was I really expected to believe that Lucy had no idea? I ground my teeth together. "Did everybody know except me?" I snapped at him.

He glanced at me, his brow furrowed. "Nobody knows about Shelby and Michael except me and you and it has to stay that way. Only

Shelby knew anything about this case before you came. Charlie dying was unexpected."

I took several deep breaths and blew them out slowly between my lips to calm my nerves.

"I was just hoping that you could poke around a bit and maybe see something that I had missed. I was really just hoping that you could figure out where the diary was and you did. I'm sorry about the rest of it. I would never put you in danger."

"That's good to know. And I did solve it, didn't I?" In a way, feeling better made me feel worse. Now I have to keep a secret from my best friends. My friends who have always been there for me. I am never going to doubt them again and I have no right to feel smug about solving the case. From now on, we are all in this together. But first I have to get permission from the ladies at the book club to include them. I guess I do keep secrets from them.

A STRANGE MOTHER

The return trip to Appleby went without issue. I was rightly chastised for ditching my friends to solve the case on my own, especially after wanting to accuse them of treating me the same way. Scott promised to get the diary to Tiffany and Audrey as soon as they were done with it. I changed into dry clothes and we caught our flight back.

No one talked much on the plane. We were all just too exhausted. My daughter Penelope was just leaving the house when Vana pulled into my driveway to drop me off. I grabbed my suitcase from the trunk and waved goodbye to her.

"Welcome back mom. How was the trip?" Penelope was bundled up in her thick jacket and gloves. The beach had been nice, but I missed the peace and quiet of the snow. The biting cold, not so much.

"It was something. Definitely not as cold as here," I added shivering as I stepped into the house. "Let's just say it was adventurous."

"Oh mom, you're not out solving crimes at the beach are you?"

"Most definitely not," I lied. "How's Chloe? And was Ginger a good girl for you?"

"They are both great. Chloe's at a friend's house right now. I'm going to pick her up. I just wanted to make sure your house was warm when you got home."

"Thanks honey." I gave her a hug and a kiss and she got in her car.

"Oh, yeah, you got a package and your mail is on the bar. I'll talk to you later."

I waved goodbye and then retrieved my luggage and purse from the car. A nice cozy fire and a hot cup of tea sounded wonderful right now.

"Ginger? Mommy's home. Where are you girl?" I dropped my keys on the table by the front door and tossed my jacket on the couch. Why wasn't Ginger greeting me at the door? "Ginger?" I called as I walked through the house. A whine greeted me as I approached my bedroom door and my heart dropped. Did Ginger get injured? Surely, my daughter would have let me know. Unless, she didn't want to ruin my vacation.

Ginger laid on her side on the bed, her tail wagging and her back to me but she didn't get up, so I crossed the room to her. "Ginger honey, what's wrong?" Worried, I hurried over and scratched her ears. "What's wrong baby?" Ginger put her nose down by her tummy and bumped it. As I looked, a tiny black kitten popped its head up and looked up at me with green button eyes and meowed sleepily. My eyebrows rose as my eyes widened.

"Where do you come from?" I wondered as I picked up the little ball of fluff. Did Penelope know about this? Naw, she would have said something. "Ginger, have you been hiding this little guy?" Ginger just whined and thumped her tail on the bed.

"Let's go get you something to eat." I carried the little guy out to the kitchen while Ginger followed my every movement like a nervous mom. I grabbed a small bowl and a little packet of tuna and let the kitten eat on the counter. The mail was there in a big pile with a small package on top. "Might as well open it first, the rest is probably just bills anyway."

I opened the cardboard box and pulled off the cotton protecting the small figurine. "Huh," was all I could think of to say because nestled in the box was a tiny baby Jesus.

WHAT'S NEXT FOR HOLLY?

A Christmas Caper

Someone is stealing Santa Claus and baby Jesus from all the Christmas displays. What could giant rooftop Santas and tiny baby Jesus' possibly have in common?

It's up to Holly, chairman of the annual Christmas Tour of Homes and her band of friends to find out who is taking them and why before the biggest fundraiser of the year gets canceled.

SIGN UP FOR MY NEWSLETTER at subscribepage.io/J9FVtd[1] and be the first to be notified when **Body at the Beach** is published. **You can check out all my books at MRDollschniederAuthor.com or join my Facebook page at**

---

1. http://subscribepage.io/J9FVtd

AUTHOR NOTES

I don't know why, but this book was so difficult to finish. I had many interruptions and found it necessary to rearrange my entire office, but the book is finally done. As with all of my stories, I love it and I look forward to writing many more adventures with Holly and the gang.

It's beautiful spring time here in the Mojave desert. Birds visit daily and my garden is coming together nicely. My husband and I spent two days and three trips into town to get supplies as it was necessary to move the garden due to dog shenanigans. Well, that and a stray adopted us that likes to dig. Fortunately, they haven't managed to knock over the nectarine tree which is currently covered with pink flowers which the bees are loving. The chickens are also apparently loving the weather as they have been giving us five eggs a day.

My husband and I also celebrated our tenth wedding anniversary on March 20th. Our anniversary gift to each other is the garden, a gift that will keep on giving. My husband thinks I'm crazy because I find pulling weeds to be therapeutic. The chickens enjoy it too because they get to eat them.

Holly's next adventure will be a Christmas Caper. I know it's spring but the story is begging to be written and I'm already 8,000 words into it.

Don't miss out!

Visit the website below and you can sign up to receive emails whenever M R Dollschnieder publishes a new book. There's no charge and no obligation.

https://books2read.com/r/B-A-QLKLB-KANFG

BOOKS 2 READ

Connecting independent readers to independent writers.